UP T' RO\

J.D.VOSE
SHELLAC PUBLICATIONS
FOREWORD

I've done a lot of things in my time in Rugby League, but never before have I been asked to write the foreword to a book.

Still, there is a first time for everything and if you derive as much pleasure from this book as I did when splitting my sides tackling endless pages of captive script then John has served a purpose.

He tells me he is just an enthusiast of the game who took his pleasure in the 40's and 50's watching players in the Greenall – Stott era at Knowsley Road. I'll tell you he has a jolly good grasp of how the game ticked in my father's time and of the good old earthy northern language and humour.

Despite the laying to rest of the cloth cap and the waistcoat and chain, following the passing of the microphone to Ray French, master of the English language and Cowley Upper 6th, by the late Eddie Waring, the book portrays life as it was in our father's and grandfathers time. It also smacks true of Rugby League even today from boardroom to dressingroom, a very down to earth approach and everybody accessible.

Even at my club, Huddersfield, there isn't a day goes by without the local council being dragged into the conversation and what appears in the book, trials and tribulations from the council chamber, is all tied in with community life.

It is compulsive reading and will surely impress my 'friends' at Chapeltown Road and make a fine addition to their ever growing library.

Also, it's got a good chance, in my opinion, of challenging the stage play 'Up And Under' should Mr. Godber and friends from the Hull Truck Company feel they can adapt it.

Alexander James Murphy

John D. Vose has written the following books.

The Lady of Connemara	Novel.
Your Feet Are Killing Me!	Humour.
Corner to Corner	Crown green bowls.
Diary of a Tramp	Life of a gentleman of the road.
The Lancashire Caruso	Life of Tom Burke, tenor.
Once a Jolly Swagman	Life of Peter Dawson. King of song.
The Statues That Moved A Nation	Miracles in Ireland.
Tales and Yarns of Glendalough and County Wicklow	Irish stories.
Collecting Old Records	Guide to 78 r.p.m. records.
Punography	The world's most obnoxious puns!

One Act Plays
> The Desirable Residence
> The Night Shelter
> Lord Bancroft's Inheritance

Three Act Plays
> A Concept of Murder   (With John Starr)
> The Minstrel Boy   A Play produced for the
>   Tom Burke centenary year.

Pantomime
> Dame Whittington and Her Dog
> Jack and the Beanstalk.

> John Vose has also Subscribed to anthologies on bowling
> and fell running.

2

Acknowledgements

My gratitude is due my son Kevin Vose, sub-editor and typesetter of The Runner magazine, for the typesetting/copy-editing. Also to John Seed for his advice and for the printing of the book. I am also grateful to John Etty, the ex-Batley, Wakefield and Oldham winger, who gave me useful background for the book; to Alex Service, the 'Saints historian', for providing me with details of playing terms for the period I have written about. My thanks also to Trevor Delaney and Robert Gate for advice and to Alex Murphy for writing the foreword. I must not forget Kathleen Snape who typed additions for the book, and that excellent artist John Dyson for the illustrations.

Also to the legions of unknown spectators who have coloured my memory with their sayings and humour on many rugby league grounds over the years.

Dedication

This book is dedicated to all those players and characters I recall with affection from my youth. Particularly Lionel Swift, the larger-than-life Saints director (who had a lot of Joshua Hepplethwaite in him!). To those 'bit' players of the game who never achieved star status but were the back bone of the code: Dilorenzo, Jimmy Lowe, 'Porky' Davies, 'Cowboy' Jones, Bert Ambler, Bill Riley, Bob Roberts, Joe Ball and company. Last, but by no means least, the late Eddie Waring, a knowledgeable and humorous man who introduced the 'up an under' and the 'early bath' to the television public.

Introduction

My love affair with rugby league began at a very early age. As a young boy I was regaled with tales of the game by my father, who was an addict. A normally mild man, on a Saturday afternoon he was transformed into the demon king of the best stand at Knowsley Road. He abused the referee, the opposition were always offside, when they scored it was from a forward pass. At Wilderspool, Brian Bevan scored several tries against Saints in a match. Dad objected to everyone of them with such vigour that there were unpleasant mutterings from the Wires' spectators. In a word, he was biased. The league code has always had its share of such characters, but they were never taken too seriously, and the days of violence on the terraces were still far away in the future. I heard stories of Alf Ellaby and George Lewis - 'I'll sing thee songs of Ellaby and tales of old George Lewis' he would warble the parody round the house; Arthur Lemmon, the welsh lad, who was astounded to find that he had been given a job in Greenalls brewery! There was Oliver Dolan, a distinguished looking chap who hooked for the Recs.; mighty Tom Barton, a fearsome three quarter who would have run through a brick wall; the Reverend Chevasse, a winger who became the Bishop of Manchester. I heard about the goal-kicking feats of Jimmy Hoey of Widnes; and the awesome footballing skills of Wagstaff and company at Fartown.

My own memories of players begin in early war time at Knowsley Road. The Fishwick brothers, Frank Balmer, Frank Tracey, Stan Powell, Albert Butler, Jack Waring, Billy French and Twist and Briscoe who perished in the war. Many players guested for opposition clubs in those wartime days. The black flyers, Cumberbatch and Francis, Fred Rule, Albert Pimblett and the legendary Jim Sullivan, prince of full-backs. The war over, my hero of them all made his mark in the game. Jimmy Stott, a tubby, homely looking centre of great ability. Opposing him, I can remember Vic Hey, the brilliant Australian, Ernest Ward, (that doyen of centres), Ernie Ashcroft of Wigan, and the flying wingers 'Jock' Johnson, Nordgren, and Alun Edwards.... memories, memories! The gigantic centre, Jack Kitching, tilting with Duggie Greenall at Odsal....Stan McCormick, dancing his way to the line.... Little Joe Ball, up-ending the gargantuan Frank Whitcombe in a torrid cup tie.....

I owe rugby league a debt, it helped to make my childhood a happy one, and has given me lots of entertainment throughout the years. I firmly believe that sport should be fun. I sincerely hope that this book will also provide fun. The story of the one-legged hooker is based on fact (believe it or not!).

My dad assured me that a Saints director was hoodwinked by a welsh chap who later revealed that he had a wooden leg!

Long may rugby league continue to thrill the crowds, may its boundaries widen, and its players never forget that they are participants in the finest sport of all. Let us hope that sophistication and modern day commercialism will never rob the game of its character.

Chapter 1

A Bad Day at Rochdale

Stanley Keighley was poking the fire in the parlour of his terraced house in Arkwright Sidings, Bramfield. It was a bitter winter's day. The street had been named after the old railway line to the defunct colliery. It was long since gone and a mountainous slagheap threatened to engulf the street at any moment. It was said to be the coldest spot in Lancashire. Clara, his wife, curlers in hair, three pairs of khaki coloured stockings encasing her spindly legs, had just finished stoning the front step with a rubbing stone given to her by the 'rag and bone man' in exchange for a pile of old dusters, and Mr Keighley's old underwear. She was now dusting a tract which hung over the parlour range. It read:

TRUST IN THE LORD AND KEEP YOUR BOWELS OPEN.

It was her father's motto. Clara was obsessed by sennapods and being a good living woman. On the opposite wall, over an ancient harmonium upon which she played hymns, hung a signed photograph of Alf Ellaby, the great winger. Stanley was proud of the fact that he was a personal friend of Alf's even though he had played for the Saints, never a popular side in Bramfield.

"Stanley lad, it's time for rugby league results", bellowed Clara, who was now black leading the grate. She may not have been the perfect wife, but she was certainly the perfect housewife. Mr Keighley, a large man of fifteen stones, sweaty feet and tartan braces, raised his corpulent backside to switch on the wireless set.

"That is the end of the rugby union results," said a voice. "Here are the rugby league results."

Hull Kingston Rovers	12	Hull	12
St.Helens Recreation	7	Castleford	5
Warrington	18	St.Helens	3
York	5	Bramley	5
Liverpool Stanley	2	Leigh	16
Broughton Rangers	15	Salford	27
Rochdale Hornets	76	Bramfield Rovers	3

Stanley Keighley smashed his fist on the parlour table and turned off the wireless in disgust.

"By the bloody hell!" he thundered.

"Language! Stanley," screeched his spouse. "I'll not have it in this 'ouse, lad, even when Rovers lose!"

"Sorry, Clara lass, but it fair makes you swear, doesn't it? Rovers beaten 73 points to 3. It's worst beating we've had since we started club. To think five year ago in 1931 we won cup. I'm ashamed to be official scout for t'club, lass".

The shock made him break wind. There was a heavy bang on the door knocker.

"Oh hecky thump!" cried Clara. "Appen it's Mr Hepplethwaite, he said he were coming after he'd been Rochdale. Open window then waft it with thee cap."

All this took some time and there was a further knock on the door.

"Anyone at home?" It *was* Mr Hepplethwaite, the chairman of Bramfield Rovers. His shoulders were covered in snow and he looked frozen to the marrow.

"Appen it were cold at Rochdale, Mr Hepplewhaite", said Clara, taking his hard hat and scraping the snow into the fire with the poker.

"Sit thee down by t'fire, I'll mash tea."

The Chairman thanked her as he warmed his hands by the welcome flames. He was a large man and towered over her husband, eighteen stones if he was an ounce, clothed in his double breasted suit which he always wore on match days, augmented tastefully by a yellow dicky bow. Normally he sported what Stanley had once described as a face as 'red as a farmer's backside on a frosty morning'. The chairman had seen great days at the club, lately the shame of defeat after defeat had reduced him to an incontinent bundle of nerves. The sudden change in temperature had set his bladder off again.

"I'm fair busting, Clara, begging your pardon, you being church, but I'm dying to go to the stone for a slash. This cold weather's making me worse than normal."

"It's a bit rocky, is basin, Mr Hepplewhaite, but it'll be alreet as long as you don't sit down." chirped Clara.

"He broke bloody thing in first place", said Stanley, when the chairman had departed down the yard.

"He's got biggest backside in Northern Union[1] has Chairman Hepplethwaite."

"Language, lad!" admonished Clara, shaking a bony finger.

"It's still a sin to say bloody, even when it's in a whisper, God can hear it. Think on, lad."

"Sorry Clara, lass." said her husband. Then his thoughts returned to his team's crushing defeat. What if old Hepplewhaite and his directors decided to sack him? Poaching union players from South Wales had paid him well, and had acted as a nice sideline to his undertaking business. The gates were so poor, he could see it happening. He could see Rovers becoming extinct. Bloody hell! He could, an all.

Besides, being a scout for a rugby league team had prestige to it. He could hold his head up high in places like Hunslet, Batley and Leigh. Not everyone could do that. He was summat of a celebrity, in fact. Money's alreet, but prestige means summat, too, aye. Some of the great players were his mates. Charlie Seeling Junior,and Hector Gee of Wigan, Billy Mercer, the old Saints' centre star. And he was on first name terms with some of the influential directors of very important clubs. His cogitative mental meanderings were interrupted by the re-emergence of the rotund chairman, who came straight to the point, as was his fashion. There was nothing devious about Joshua.

"You'll be worrying about your job now, Stanley lad?"

By the cram, he was going to get his notice, that was it. That massive defeat had put the kibosh on it well and truly. The chairman's words had the sting of a whip lash, the thud of a boot on leather, the cruel screech of a referee's whistle. He'd pretend to ignore it, for the moment. Take it on the chin, like Peter Kane, the Goldborne lad.

"Tuck thee shirt in, Mr Hepplewhaite, my Clara's a bit religious, tha knows. Always do thee buttons up after tha's been lavvy, she says. It seems her great uncle Septimus, on her mother's side, once went to see Little Tich at Wigan Hippodrome. He laughed so much, he busted his fly buttons, and he were done for indecent explosion, it was a mark of shame on family."

"Stanley", said Mr Hepplewhaite, tucking in his shirt. "I've come here to talk rugby league, not to reminisce about Clara's great uncle Septimus and his faulty flies.....but I can see you're playing for time, trying to change subject, lad. But man to man, and seeing your Clara's in back parlour, mashing tea, I'm peeing so often it's not *worth* buttoning up. Doctor says it's all worry over Rovers what's doing it, and I might have to have me probate gland removed. But keep that under your hat, think on. Keep it private, like.... hee hee, that were an unintentional pun, weren't it. Does get it?"

"I'm gad my Clara didn't hear it or you'd have got it!"

"Sod your Clara, she's too holy for her own good. Take her to New Brighton for ride on big dipper, and a bit of slap an' tickle in park bushes....oh, hello again Clara..." The Chairman tried to rise, but his backside stuck fast between the arms of the fireside chair. Her face told him she had heard his ribaldry.

"I were brought up proper, Mr Hepplewhaite, and I don't like suggestive talk in my own parlour."

But for all Clara's sanctimonious ways, she was mad on rugby league. To her, Featherstone Rovers were far more exciting than Rudolf Valentino. Her Father had dreamed of having a boy who would play for Bramfield Rovers. He'd refused to buy her a doll for christmas, and instead she was given a miniature rugby ball. That was the start of a love affair with the club which was consummated when she met Stanley Keighley in the Supporters' club hut over a cup of tea and a barm cake. Rumour had it that it was the only thing that was consummated, for as everyone in Bramfield knew, Clara Keighley had been brought up proper. Now she was gazing out of the window at the falling snow.

"Eee, poor lass", she muttered. "It's poor old Mrs Kelly wheeling a bassinet full of coal waste from tip. She'll not get much warmth out of that stuff. I'll just go and have a word with t'lass, and see if I can do owt

10

for her, while tea's brewing."

"She's a good hearted lass, is Clara. But she can be a bit tetchy an all." said the chairman when she had departed. "Mind you, I feel all on edge me sell, worst day of me life, it were, Stanley. You were lucky it were your day for collecting for burial club, or you'd have seen t'funeral of the Rovers if you'd come Rochdale. And them a team as we've annihilated....aye, annihilated! .....On many occasions in past. If it were' Uddersfield or Leeds I wouldn't feel so bad, but to be beaten by t'Hornets by that score is hard to swallow. Even though we were playing on their midden. I don't think it would have been any different if we'd been at home, mind you, the way we played. I felt proper humiliated, and so did my co-directors. That toffee-nosed chairman of theirs, who speaks with a plum in his mouth, he comes up to us at half-time and says "Will't join us for a cup of tea, gentlemen, with some whisky in it? Or would you sooner lace it with arsenic?"

Reet sarcastic, he were. Every time t'Hornets scored, their directors jumped up and down like a gang of howling dervishes. And for once in me life, I didn't blame ref. In fact, I think he were a bit lenient on Rovers and let 'em off a few infringements."

"It's a cold spot is Rochdale" remarked Stanley.

"Cowd? It were like Siberia, and that ruddy best stand of theirs has got more holes in it than a colander. It fair played up me chilblains, as if I haven't got enough problems. By the way, Stanley, does know any cure for 'em.....? Your old dad were a great one for old fashioned Lancashire cures, when he were alive, if I remember reet."

"He were an all," agreed Stanley. "Soak thee feet in lant[2], it's best thing for chill blains. Tha's got plenty of that Mr. Chairman."

The chairman took the joke well. "By the cram, I have an all, lad."

Stanley had more to add on the subject of cures.

"Some Lancashire people used to drink it, me dad told me, it purified the blood. Cumfrie's another good remedy, more for sprains, though, I think. Do you remember old Cuddy Pembleton, who trained the team after the First War? He swore by Cumfrie. He grew it in his his allotment, especially for the club. He reckoned it were finest thing out for bruises and swellings. And he used to sup a gill for his supper, before going bed. He lived till he were 96, did Cuddy. He'd got such bony hands, players were frightened of getting injured, in case he had

11

to rub them down."

Joshua chuckled at the memory.

"He'd turn in his grave would old Cuddy if he saw the team we have now. He'd have more chance of training a bunch of monkeys. Although I shouldn't be unkind, they do their best."

"We'll have to stop the band playing t'Entry of the Gladiators, when players run out, it makes speccies laugh and hoot." said Stanley.

"Your reet." agreed the chairman. "Dance Of The Sugar Plum Fairies would be more appropriate."

The key turned in the front door. "Look out! She's back", said Stanley.

Clara poured the tea for the two dejected Rovers men, She felt their sadness,and shared it. "It's bad, Mr Hepplethwaite, isn't it? Even old Mrs Kelly was talking about it. You'd think she had enough worries, poor old wench. It just shows you what Rovers means to folk in Bramfield."

Joshua gave her a comforting pat on the back, with a flabby hand.

"I feel proper sorry for die-hard speccies who've followed us through thick and thin. All best players sold to make ends meet, and lots of so called supporters taking their hooks like rats off a sinking ship. Some speccies are fickle folk." Joshua took a mouthful of hot tea before continuing. "They want a winning team, and that is their right. After all, in a town like ours there's enough losers, what with depression. There's enough gloom and misery. It bucks folks up when team wins, and reverse applies when we are at wrong end of a thrashing, week in, week out. We've all got to pull us belts in drastically at the club."

This was Clara's chance. Although she was a fanatical supporter, she loved her brass, too.

"I know it's no concern of mine, Mr Hepplethwaite, but is it really bad? Are the rumours true? Is the club going to close down?"

Joshua emptied the remains of his tea into his saucer and sucked it up noisly. "You're entitled to ask, Clara. The blunt answer is, we're sinking fast. Only hope is the council. But it will be a hard job to get brass out of them. As you know, I'm on council, and I'll have a good try. It comes up on agenda on Monday."

As Joshua spoke, Clara was nudging her husband, who knew she was wanting him to ask the chairman about his job as scout, for which he was paid a monthly retainer. But Stanley couldn't bring himself to ask the question, even though the chairman had already referred to it. But Clara had no qualms. "What about my Stanley, is his job safe?"

"None of us jobs is safe, Clara. Not Stanley's, not mine, or my co-directors, and not the club's secretary, either. We're doing some severe pruning. There was some straight talking on way back from t'Hornets match today. There's very little money for wages. Church mouse couldn't be worse of than us at moment. So I've got to ask your husband if he'll do without his retainer for a couple of months."

"What, go off scouting beawt brass?" Clara was appalled.

"It's no use scouting for players when we've no brass to buy 'em with, face facts, lass. Blunt truth is we can't afford to pay 'em. We're skint", said Joshua.

"So that's all the thanks he gets, is it? My husband's been a good scout for Rovers. Look at all welshmen he's brought up north. Tell him lad, stand up for thee sell!"

"Aye, I will an all." said Stanley, who usually needed a push from his wife

"Club's had its moneys worth out of me", he began, suitably encouraged.

"No-one's saying otherwise, lad." said Joshua.

"I've brought some belting welsh talent up to Bramfield. I'm known as the plague of the valleys, down there. There were Bert Jones, Cliff Jones, Granville Jones, Edgar Price-Jones, Dai Morgan, Dai Prosser and his brother Bert, Dai Nugent, Wynn Davies, Dai Owen, Joe Francis, Fred Trotter, Syd Llewellyn, Morgan Judd, Islwyn Tranter, Cliff Watkins, Glynn Harrison, Ted Reece and his Brother Dai, Eric Walters, the flying winger, Watt Jenkins, Ivor Jenkins....."

"Alreet, alreet, we don't want the litany of the saints", interrupted the chairman.

"What's St.Helens got to do with it? I'm talking about Rovers, not Knowsley Road."

"I don't mean them saints, muffin yed! I mean saints in heaven."

"We're strict methodist here, we don't know about them catholic things." said Clara. Her sanctimonious attitude annoyed the chairman.

"What the heck's religion got to do with it, Clara? We all come out of same pot, black men, yellow men, Jews, and genitals, they're all welcome here. Why, we even take Yorkshire men. Anyroads up, we know what you've done for club, Stanley, they were all good uns, there's no denying it. My co-directors, Bert and Bob Kearsley, were only saying same thing on way home from match....but you've let a few slip through your fingers, owd cock. Don't forget that. Gus Risman went to Salford, when you assured us he was coming t'Bramfield. And you turned that young Alun Edwards down, cos you said he were all skin and bone.....what a flyer he's proving to be for the Red Devils. And what about butter fingers Bailey, what you got from Oldham way? You told us he was another Rosenfeld, kept grabbing at ball with one hand, couldn't take a pass proper. Only played a handful of first team games. Hee hee, that were a good tale about him going to labour exchange for a job. It was when folk were emigrating on assisted passages. The clerk asked him would he go to Australia, and Bailey told him he'd go if he were picked! World's greatest optimist. You bought us a duck egg, that time."

"No-one's perfect", mumbled Stanley. "I pinched many a good un under noses of big clubs, including Salford. Don't you forget that, Mr Hepplethwaite. And don't you forget the local talent that I've found.. Bob Oxley, Percy Aspinall, Jim Thistlethwaite, Jimmy Scott - he was an international, were Jimmy....".

"You've made your point, lad. You can quote names till your red in face, but it won't alter the fact that your services won't be needed in a crisis. That's not my decision, Stanley, it's a decision made by a higher authority - fate. If we do survive - and it'll be an act of escapology worthy of Houdini if we do – then we'll need you again. All I'm asking you to do is to forego a couple of months' brass."

Joshua had to leave the room again.

"He fair looks peaky, does lad." said Clara.

"Aye, he's not well isn't Mr Hepplewhaite, appen he needs a double whisky to warm him up. I could do with one and all, after the news we've had."

"You'll not have it in my 'ouse, Stanley Keighley - think on. Drink is a curse. The ruin of the working classes."

"It makes you curse, when you can't have it." moaned Stanley.

"Tell thee what, Stanley, nip down cellar and get a bottle of auntie Mary Alice's rhubarb wine. Appen that'll cheer him up a bit, i'm partial to a drop meself."

auntie Mary Alice, an' all. I remember her when she was a cotton queen. Miss Shuttle 1922 she were."

Clara helped them all to another glass each. That's her fifth, thought Stanley to himself. Surely he'd get his conjugations tonight. The chairman was still grinning at him. Stanley saw red, and nearly choked on a piece of thick, seamy tripe.

"I'll make you and rest of committee laugh on t'other side of your faces. I'll consult a solicitor, I will an' all. Being a league scout isn't easy, I've nearly been beaten up a few times. I've had to wear a disguise on some grounds where I'm known, bought it out of me own pocket and never charged club for it."

"It would look well on balance sheet - false beards and red noses for t'scout!" laughed Joshua.

Stanley was not amused. "It's no laughing matter. A scout needs 'danger money' going down to Wales. One chap threatened to kill me if I took any more promising talent from valleys. They hate professionals, do the administrators, but the folks down there are more like us up here. Working class. I'll never forget that trip I made down to watch Harlequins versus Wasps. It's worse in them places 'cos they're all money'ed folk, 'an I've heard tell that if a player signs for league, he gets ostrich-eyed by his family and all his mates, so you can imagine what they thought of me when they discovered I was a league scout. I should never have asked for Lancashire hot pot in club house, it gave the game away. They treated me like vermin, and one bloke chased me off premises with a shooting stick, and another threatened to set his hounds on me if I ever appeared again."

"Well, it serves you right", said Joshua. "You shouldn't go south of Leicester, it's indian country down there. English rugby union's never been a great gathering ground for the league. Upper class hooligans I call 'em."

"Aye, it's a good brain and a quick pair of heels you want in my line. I'm a cross between Sherlock Holmes and a whippet with its bloody backside on fire."

"Language! In our house, too."

"Oh, give over, Clara! I'll swear in my own house if I wants, I've got my livelihood to think of wi' Rovers going down plug-oile. Mind you, I've got my undertaker's business to fall back on."

"An that's not what it were since Co-op started giving divvy on burials." sympathised his wife.

"You're right, Clara lass. And offering two for price of one has hit me hard, and all."

"I bet it has. It's not fair encouraging folk to die in pairs, it's not christian." added Joshua, then unable to prevent another almighty guffaw, he said "Trade's dead, is it?"

It was received with a silence as deadly as the subject they were discussing. "It were only my little joke," he explained. "A pun, it was..... a play on words..... "

Clara rapped at him. "Dying's not a joking subject. Besides, that joke's as old as t'hills. If anyone jokes about death in this house, it's Mr Keighley - my husband - it's his purgative being t'undertaker. He's buried nobility, has Mr Keighley."

"Appen dying's spreading to the club. They play like warmed up corpses." said Joshua. "But cheer up, Stanley. Who knows, a miracle might happen and things'll get better. My committee appreciates all you've done for club, and as for funeral business, that'll never stop. There's folk dying now what's never died before."

"Appen so", said the scout seriously. He wouldn't have got a joke if it had turned up in Rovers' colours waving a rattle. The meal was at an end, and Joshua gave his mouth and double chins a good wiping with a polka dot handkerchief.

"If you go to heaven Clara, you'll be in charge of the catering." He told her warmly.

"What do you mean, *if*? Good living folk all go there, that's what I were brought up to believe."

"Quite so,..... slip of the tongue, lass... I meant *when*, of course. Oh, by the way, Stanley, I've just remembered something. We want you to do us a favour next Saturday. We're away at St Helens. City Road that is, we're playing the Recs. Ruddy big rough forrards they are 'an all."

"What do you want me to do? Turn out for you? It's not come to that, has it?"

"Nay lad, although you'd make a good stop-gap forrard, being built like a brick W.C. We're having to pull us horns in, all roads, so we're taking the team in cars to play the Recs. It's not a long journey, we've got two lined up, but we want another. Can you loan us one of your

18

funeral limousines?"

"They're not mine, Mr Chairman. I hire them from a taxi firm. The only one that belongs to me is the hearse. But you'll not want that?"

"Why not? We can't be fussy in our predicament. Remove anything that happens to be in it, and we'll put cushions down. You can drive it."

"But won't the players get stiff?" queried Clara.

"I reckon it's had stiffer passengers." said Joshua.

Stanley nodded his consent. "Alreet, but I'm not driving up to the ground in it, they'll have to walk last quarter of a mile. I'll park it a bit out of way. St. Helens cemetry is only up the road from t'ground."

Agreement having been reached, and arrangements for collection of the players decided upon, Clara said she would play the harmonium. It was an idyllic scene, one to warm the hearts of exiled northerners in the far flung regions of the world, from St.Albans to Baghdad. Saturday evening in a warm parlour after a good 'tuck in', with a sing-song to finish off, a pleasant prospect indeed; but Clara's choice of music was hardly of the sing - along variety. Oh Let Me Like A Soldier Fall, and The Heart Bowed Down with Weight Of Woe, were her party pieces, which she attacked with a vocal fervour worthy of Prince Monolulu[3] shouting out tips at Haydock Park.

Joshua loved a good sing-song with the lads on the way home from a match in the chara' as it chugged over Blackstone Edge, or on a long bleak haul over the Cumberland hills after a match at Barrow.

"She's got a very extensive musical reservoir, has Clara." remarked Stanley.

"Appen she has, lad." mumbled Joshua, who immediately fell into a deep slumber, from which all the doleful music in the world would not have awoken him. He'd had enough sadness for one day.

ROVERS PLAYERS BOUND FOR ST. HELENS

Chapter Two

Joshua Sets Out To Save T'Rovers

Joshua Parkinson Hepplethwaite, to give him his baptismal name, lived about a mile away from Bramfield town centre. Being the proprietor of a local linen sheet mill, he was 'well heeled', to quote an expression often used about the Rovers' chairman, and he was the main shareholder in the club. He loved his 'brass' like any hardened northerner, but he loved his rugby league more. If the club was to fold up, he would not only lose his money but his life blood as well. Naturally jovial, his manner usually flamboyant, he was a friend to all classes in the town. His employees loved him, but his blunt manner was often too much to stomach by those people who considered themselves a cut above the rest. There was 'nowt' false about Joshua. If he had enemies then they were more likely to be his equals, business people and members of the council probably jealous of his popularity. There were richer men in the town but certainly there were none more popular than 'Jovial Josh' as he was sometimes known. He loved to hand out his business cards with gay abandon.

Joshua Hepplethwaite
The Biggest Sheet House In Bramfield

If the linen business had hit lean times he could have taken it on his two double chins, but his beloved Rovers, never..... it was a blow to the heart, a stab to the jugular, a thrust to the vitals. It hurt deeply and it showed. It was now an effort to be cheerful, anxiety had furrowed his brow, it was hard for him to prevent his bright personality from being dulled by circumstance. Never more than that Monday evening as he stood in front of the hall mirror surveying his wan features and fixing his bowler hat at a jaunty angle. He felt more like going to bed. He was weary. He had worked from being twelve years of age in the mills, finding prosperity by the sweat of his brow and he had never felt tired. This worry was a killer, he was feeling ill and worn out for the first time in his life. The doctor had told him to exercise more, to lose weight. He had tried walking to the factory but the urgent desire to pass water which assailed him at frequent intervals was a constant worry. As anyone who has had 'waterworks trouble' will tell you, the more you worry about it the more you want to pee. He had planned his walk to the Town Hall over his tea. A walk anywhere these days was hazardous since the bladder trouble had raised its ugly head. To think he should be worried about walking down the street, it was an indication of his nervous state and general feeling of anxiety. How things had changed. He had thought nothing of leading the lads out at Wembley. He would go down Gasworks Street and that would lead him to the back door of the Town Hall.

It was Mr Hepplethwaite at the rugby club but he was Councillor when he was in town. He disliked being in local government. He was too straight and open for that sort of thing, and had only joined so he could help the club and foster rugby league in the town. It was nice to meet folk and have them ask about t'Rovers, or it had been until they had become the chopping block for all the other teams in the league.....72 points to 3 at Rochdale Hornets, of all teams! He felt ashamed. Humiliated. He didn't relish the other remarks, however, regularly made by women who thought all their problems were the responsibility of the council, and that he alone was capable of putting all their complaints to right. He was on his way now to an important meeting at the Town Hall to try to save the club. Clad in his warm crombie overcoat, he crossed the canal bridge. A couple of lads in short pants, which almost reached to their ankles, were fishing for jack sharps by the light of a gaslamp with pins on the end of string. One lucky lad even had a fishing net, a sign of wealth in Bramfield. Joshua gazed down at the dirty water full of old prams and tin cans. That was a mistake, the sight of water made him want to go. Blast his probate! He cussed to himself. Fortunately no-one was looking as he added his offering to the already vile waters of the canal.

Viaduct Street was notorious at the Town Hall for complaining women, but the one consolation was that it was a short street. He walked along it as fast as his bulk would allow. Amazingly, he got to the end without anyone accosting him about dirty middens or dead cats in the back alley. Heaving a huge sigh of relief he waddled across Marsh's field, where kids where playing tick rugby with a 'ball ' made out of old newspapers and elastic bands. He gave the lads a quick look, but his heart wasn't in it, he was thinking about what lay ahead at the Town Hall meeting. "Come on, Joshua lad", a little voice spoke inside him." You always watched out for local talent, remember how you found Jimmy Franks playing with a stuffed bladder over on Houghton's tip". He did remember, Jimmy Franks had been a winner for Bramfield until they'd had to sell him to Leeds to pay debts. Bloody Leeds! He hated them..... tempting all good lads from poorer clubs, and even fixing them up with jobs. Bramfield Rovers couldn't compete with influential sides like them, and he hated Wigan as well and Salford, but at least they were Lancashire clubs. The little voice won so Joshua went closer to the group of would be rugby stars who were arguing amongst themselves. Arguing 'toss' as they say in Lancashire. A little carrot haired lad was yelling "my team's Wigin, my team's Wigin. Up the Ham Rags!"

"We're 'Uddersfield, claret and gold", said one of the opposition.

"That's were t'Yorkshire cow comes from" piped up carrot head.

"What does mean, Yorkshire cow?" asked one of his mates.

"It wouldn't have it's udders feeled, does get it?"

"You better not let yer mam hear you say that, Tommy, she might tell priest at school."

"You can't be Uddersfield, any road, you were them last week.

You've got to be a different team every time we play, then we can write results down and have a league."

"That's a belting idea", said a lad with a runny nose and no seat in his trousers. "Let's be Bramfield Rovers, instead".

An announcement that the Sadlers Wells ballet company was coming to Bramfield Hippodrome instead of Frank Randal's 'Scandals' couldn't have caused more disgust and vocal objection. Runny nose was ridiculed by his team mates. One of them shouted:

"What, them lot of bakes? I'd sooner play soccer like cissies do than be Rovers. I'm gooing wom, and I'm taking ball with me, it's mine." The owner of the ball, always the most important player on the field in kids' tick rugby matches, strolled away with his proud possesion.

"We won Wembley once." said runny nose stoically.

Carrot head blew a raspberry in ridicule. "Aye, that's history now. My dad blames committee and that chairman. He reckons our cat could do a better job. They couldn't run a chip shop. My dad says he wouldn't pay any of players with washers..... I tell thee what, why don't you be Hull Kingston Rovers, Billy?"

"What, Yorksheer? Nay, I'd sooner be Swinton A team."

Carrot head was determined to do a thorough assassination job on the Rovers. "My dad says they couldn't beat girls' school. He calls Rovers' pack the easy six. Right puddins, they are an all....."

Joshua could stand no more. He sidled away as the debate intensified, a tear wetting his cheek. Well....he wasn't really surprised, he was no stranger to criticism. He'd heard it all before, and said the same things when he was a lad. He knew all about the short memories and the equally short tempers of many spectators. They ebbed and flowed like the tide at Blackpool. Quick to write in to the Bramfield Trumpet accusing the directors of picking the wrong players and committing all the sins directors the world over are said to commit. You had to turn a blind eye and have a hard skin like referees. Most clubs have their bad times, he told himself. But to hear kids blabbing it out like that! But a lot of it was true. It was the worst Rovers' team of all time. Worst team in the league. He knew that it was no fault of his, or his co-directors, the Kearsley brothers. But they would be blamed all the same, that was the code. Someone had to carry the proverbial can. Whatever he did, he must never give the impression that he was dejected, head high and keep in good spirits....but eee, it were bloody hard, an all! He was starkly aware of the reality of the team's financial plight, and speccies could never really understand. What's more, they didn't want to know. They didn't care a tuppenny damn. It were results they wanted. Praising you one minute and shouting abuse the next. Fair weather friends, speccies. But then wasn't that speccies the world over? Aye....he consoled himself, "Speccies the world over".

As he walked the gamut of this dingy street of soul destroying yellow brick, he was hit in the eye by a large piece of floating chemical waste from the works across the canal cutting. Although it was well past finishing time at the factory, its putrid output still hung in the air above the town waiting to be deposited in the face of a passing town dweller by the sadistic quirk of a gust of wind. Goblets of foul excreta. This stuff even disgusted Joshua. He was used to coal tips and slag heaps, dilapidated mill houses that had once housed mill workers until the depression had closed them; also he knew it was a northern working class town, and as such it could never pretend to be a garden city, but nowadays you could almost smell the poverty and the hopelessness in the town. No-one expected much else in Bramfield, these days. They would put up with anything if only they had work. They were proud hard working folk, but they deserved better. It was bad enough to live in a stinking place of belching chimneys laden with lung destroying smoke and chemical filth, many of the folk gaunt and ghost-like in complexion, it would be worse when the rugby mad inhabitants lost their team.... aye, that goblet of floating muck said it all. It were a slap in the teeth..... a kick in the privates to a dying man. Wasn't the bloody place grim enough? As if this wasn't bad enough, the vile stench from the gasworks would have made a navvy vomit. No wonder the town was disparagingly referred to as the arsehole of England.

"Oh sod it!" breathed Joshua

"Here comes Miss flaming Shawllcross. She'd frighten Smith[4] Fildes and Mulvaney, would that lass!"

The thin weedy figure of a notorious gossiping harridan waylaid him with a closed umbrella. She stunk of moth balls, and was known to everyone as 'Acid Alice'.

"So we do see you sometimes,Councillor."

"Good evening, Miss Shawllcross, it's clement for time of year." "Never mind the pleasantries Councillor, what about my midden? I were down at Town Hall and a young fella wrote my midden down in a big book, but nowts been done about it. Bottom's burned out of it with hot ash and that flash woman that lives over t'brush with a chinese sailor from Leigh keeps filling it up with unmentionables."

"I geet a monkey out of Exchange and Mart, Councillor." To avoid the haranguing of Miss Shawllcross, Joshua had turned away only to find himself addressed by a spindly fellow in clinic glasses.

"You what, young man?" said the harassed councillor.

"I geet a monkey out of Exchange and Mart".

"And what's that got to do with me, young man?"

"It had a gammy leg, I reckon it got damaged at Crewe on station. It were a man from Cornwall what sent it, and I paid him good money, an all. Can council sue him on my behalf, Councillor? Should I put a complaint in to Town Hall?"

"Aye, lad, aye, do that", said Joshua gladly, but his escape was cut off by two large busted women in coloured aprons and henna hairnets. One was holding a rolling pin. Both were built like prop forwards.

"Kids are knocking on doors again, Councillor Hepplethwaite." said the woman in the green pinny.

"And they're at rope trick again, an all. They want thumping. I blame wireless for it. I keep going to Town Hall, but nothing gets done. You know what I mean by rope trick, Councillor, don't yer?"

Mr H nodded, he knew it well. He had done it himself when he was a kid. Every door in Gasworks street had a large shiny knob on it. They were useful for pulling the door when you were closing it. The idea was to tie a piece of rope to one door and fasten tightly to the knob on the door of the next house. Gasworks Street being all terraced houses with no gardens made it very easy to do the rope trick.

"What's matter, Councillor? Tha looks a bit on peaky side." It was the woman in the turquoise pinny and the scarlet lipstick.

"Well, as a matter of fact, Mrs Muldoon, I'd like to use your back lavvy, if you don't mind. I'm off to council meeting, and I better go before I gets theer."

"Certainly, Councillor." said Mrs Muldoon. "Come through parlour and you can go through back yard. Don't trip over cat, it's had kittens. My Michael, God rest his soul, suffered from being taken short too. Doctor told him it were inconsequence."

Joshua needed no guiding to the lavatory at the bottom of the back yard. He had been born in a similar house himself, so the stink of tom cats and the even worse stench from the midden didn't effect his nostrils in the same way it would have done to more sensitive mortals. Relief was engulfing his vitals when there was a rat-a-tatting on the door.

"When's tha's finished what yer doing, can yer take notice of state of flags in yard? It's time council were sending someone round to cement 'em....." There was a monentary pause as Mrs Muldoon thought of another complaint.

"And by the way, Councillor, I'm not being rude, like, but if you sit down you'll see the holes in roof above your head. My Michael, God rest him, used to count the stars. He reckoned he learnt more about the galaxy sitting on that seat than he did at library. You'll tell 'em at council, won't yer?"

Joshua had a brain wave. He would go out of the backyard gate and follow the snicket almost down to the Town Hall. Surely no-one would accost him now? But escape was not easy. He had only progressed about twenty yards when a mop of peroxide blonde hair thrust itself over the top of a wall. It was the woman who lived over the brush with the chinese sailor from Leigh. She was well known to Joshua as a grumbler and a grouser.

"I thought it was you, Mr Hepplethwaite. I want to make an official complaint about my next door neighbour, at no 26. She's making my life a misery....lend me this....lend me that.... lend me t'other..... bit o' butter, bottle o' milk, a cup of sugar, local paper..... You name it, she's wanting to borrow it. Last week, she came to the door, and asked if she could borrow the Sunday joint to make a bit of gravy....."

"Put it in writing.", said Councillor Hepplethwaite. That was always a good get-out. "Aye, do that lass, then it goes through proper channels." If he knew the Town Hall, it would go down lavvy, but it got him out of a tough spot.

"I've got arthuritus in me wrist, but I'll get our kid to do it." But by this time, Joshua was out of earshot, and passing the little Bethel chapel with the rusty tin roof. The sound of a tenor voice took his mind off the mundane things of life. He knew the song well. He stopped by the gate to listen. It was the aria, Lend Me Your Aid, from The Queen of Sheba, by Gounod.

It was his dad's favourite, and he could remember him playing it on the old horn gramophone in the front parlour. What a song for a man in his position. He needed the council's aid, but he hated having to ask for it. He had too many enemies, too many folk were jealous of him, even though he was from working class roots, like themselves. That

27

little voice inside him was at it again... "Why not get the churches to pray for Rovers?" Aye, why not? He remembered, how back in 1930 when lowly Widnes played St.Helens, team of all the talents, at Wembley, prayer was said to have won the day for the 'Chemics'. Most of the Widnes team were catholics, and the local nuns took it upon themselves to bombard heaven..... fantasy or whatever, it worked.... Saints, with Alf Frodsham, Fairclough, Hall and the rest of the stars were given the run around by the `Chemics`, the biggest surprise ever in the cup final.

When he arrived at the bottom of the snicket, the tenor started on Count Your Blessings. That was rubbing it in. Appen the council would give their blessing to the stricken club, he thought. It was an anthem of hope, perhaps? Joshua was tempted to nip in to a 'local' for a brandy, to give him extra confidence to face the council, but he resisted. He was sure of one vote, anyway. Councillor Heneberry, the supporters' club chairman, would vote for him, and he had been trying to persuade other councillors to support Joshua. Instead of the drink, he had a walk around the police yard at the rear of the town hall, going over in his mind all the salient points he needed to present to the council. The club's future depended upon his eloquence and powers of persuasion. He thought about those kids playing tick rugby on the wasteland. They were the future. If he failed to save the Rovers, there would be no rugby league for them to support in the town. He owed it to them to pull the club through, to give them a team they could be proud of, and perhaps even play for. His mind travelled back to Wembley and the adulation they had received. Naturally, a lot of the glory had rubbed off on him, and he felt understandably proud. How the wheel had turned! One day you're up, and the next you're down. The strident notes of the town hall clock struck seven. He entered the door leading to the council chamber, for once in his life in a nervous state. He knew now what players meant when they talked about butterflies in the stomach before big games. This was the biggest match he would ever take part in.

Chapter 3

The Council Meeting

In the Town Hall chamber stood a large table covered with red leather. Fourteen councillors, all male, sat round it waiting for the chairman to call the meeting to order. Councillor Wiggins was talking to Albert Heneberry about Joshua Hepplethwaite.

"He's not looking too well lately, isn't lad. I reckon it's his sphincter what's causing trouble."

"I didn't know Joshua had been to Egypt." said Councillor Heneberry.

"What the hell's Egypt got to do with it?" asked Councillor Wiggins.

"It's what they have there in t'pyramids, thar knows.....You know the old saying, 'as inscrutable as a sphincter', don't you?"

"Oh bloody hell! I would have to sit next to thee, Albert." whispered Councillor Wiggins to himself. "I never know if he's serious or taking piss."

"I reckon it's his bladder." suggested old Councillor Gorman.

"Nay, Lad. I think it's his water works." said the councillor next to him.

"Look out, here he comes." said Councillor Wiggins, which set up a barrage of embarrassed coughing, because all present knew there was going to be a dog-fight when the question of Rovers came on the agenda. Joshua negotiated his expansive frame into a chair and waited for the meeting to be called to order.

There is nothing more boring on this earth than listening to the secretary reading the minutes of the last meeting. Joshua groaned and squirmed as he listened to the doleful monotone of the secretary as he read from a red leather book. It seemed impossible that they had discussed so many items at the last meeting. Joshua could see the Town Hall clock. The secretary had begun to read at seven minutes past seven and it was now 7.25. At last he sat down. Old Charlie Pye had started to snore and whistle through his teeth. All this was aggravating Joshua's nerves.

"Knock him!" snapped Councillor Crumpsall, the chairman of the committee. Charlie Pye was stone deaf and could only hear when he used his tin ear trumpet. He never used it for boring bits like minutes of the last meeting, and invariably fell asleep.

"Is it time for tea?" blurted old Charlie, stirring from his slumber.

"We've only just read minutes! Pay attention!" shouted Jeremiah Crumpsall, who was as nasty as a bag of tom cats.

"I must have been in th'arms of Morpheus." explained Charlie.

"I'd sooner be in th'arms of that blonde wench what they've got at Bull and Bracket." said Councillor Heneberry. "I bet she's a hot 'un!"

"We'll have no smut, Councillor." barked the chairman. "This is a God-fearing council, and I must ask you to moderate your language. Thar's not at home, thar knows. Now, to the next item on agenda. I have a proposition from Councillor Small to purchase a gondola for the lake in Fletcher Park. He reckons the boats do good business and bring us in a lot of revenue. It could be a good idea. Have we a seconder? What about you, Councillor Pye? Can you hear me?"

"You what?" came the answer. Councillor Crumpsall raised his voice.

"I said will you *second* the motion?"

"You what?"

"Have a look at his ear trumpet, somebody, it's probably bunged up. He'll have to go, you know."

An obliging councillor gently removed the ancient ear trumpet from old Charlie's ear and up-ended it on the table. A Mint Imperial fell out.

"Well, I'll go to our 'ouse." shrieked Charlie. "I were sucking that and I thought as I'd swallowed it.........er...what were you saying, Mr Chairman?"

"We want a seconder to Councillor Small's proposition to purchase a gondola for the park lake. Will you second the proposition?"

"Aye, of course I will." agreed Charlie. " But why not get two and then we can breed off 'em?"

30

"Item two." announced the chairman, ignoring old Charlie. "It has been proposed by Councillor Percy Hawkins that we have a new urinal erected in the park. The existing one has been there since the park opened, and is now in a very dilapidated state. We have had complaints from many park users and from fishermen. Dr. O'Brien, Medical Officer of Health, has inspected the site, and is of the opinion that it is a health hazard. What's more, we have lost six Silver Carp, three Roach, four Pike, two Perch, nine Rudd and seven Gudgeon. Not to mention, a whole host of small fry. It would appear, according to my report, that urinals are leaking into the lake. It also states that many of the ducks are staggering about in a distressed state......."

"Probably pissed." suggested Councillor Heneberry.

"I heard that, Councillor! Out, off thee go!"

Jeremiah pointed a bony finger at the miscreant that made him look for all the world like a referee giving marching orders to a stand-off who had just thumped his rival in the kidneys.

"It were nowt," protested the joker. "nowt at all."

"Foul language is objectionable in the council chamber. I warned thee only a few minutes ago. Off thee go and sit in Green Room until it's tea break, and think on thy've been warned. It'll go in minutes........think on, Mr Secretary, record it. You know as well as I do that I have the power as chairman of council to expel anyone from a meeting who uses objectionable language."

The disgraced councillor left the room muttering something about sactimonious old goats. Albert Heneberry was noted for being the council wag. He owned a chemist's sundries firm and specilaised in making haemorrhoid ointment which folks said had made him a lot of money. 'Piles of it' as Albert liked to state. He'd had the place in uproar with his jokes and crude remarks so often that the chairman had made up his mind to exercise his perogative of expulsion.

"He's going for an early bath, Joshua." remarked old Gormley, but Joshua was in no mood for comical references to rugby league.

"Now, back to business." said Jeremiah, almost seeming to gloat over his masterly use of officialdom within the chamber.

"Have we any comments on the subject of urinals? What about you, Councillor Bagley? You're on the parks and gardens.... what do you think about a new urinal in Fletcher Park?"

'UP T' ROVERS!'
AND 'UP T' BLOODY COUNCIL

The aforesaid Bert Bagley hated difficult questions. It always seemed to him that Jeremiah Crumpsall loved to put him on the spot. It was obvious to Councillor Wiggins that Bert was stumped, so he whispered to him quite audibly that a urinal was where you went to relieve yourself when taken short.

"Oh, I see," said Bert eagerly. "Good idea Mr Chairman, and while we're at it why not get an arsenal as well?"

The sound of the Salvation Army band broke upon the meeting from the street below to flood the council chamber. It was one of Chairman Crumpsall's favourite hymns. He held up his hand. "Lets listen for a few moments, gentlemen. We've had gutter language so lets have a bit of sacred music to purify council chamber, so to speak. You can sing if you wish."

Old Charlie piped up in a screeching voice reminiscent of a castrated ferret. This was even too much for Jeremiah who hammered on the table with his gavel.

"That's enough, on with business!"

He allowed himself a side glance at Joshua Hepplethwaite who he knew was inwardly raging. He was well aware that Joshua disliked him and the feeling was mutual.

"Bloody delaying tactics." muttered Johua to his neighbour. "Hypo-critical old beggar, he'll do owt to put off business of Rovers until last second."

Mind you, he had expected there would be a lot of business before the question of aid to the ailing rugby club came up. Crumpsall hated sport, and in particular rugby league. It was common knowledge that he had only been married for eighteen months when his bride ran off with a scrum-half from Salford. Furthermore, she'd been playing away for months before she was caught offside. Up to then, Jeremiah had been a season ticket holder at Rovers but cancelled it when the news of his wife's unfaithfulness hit the town. He swore vengeance on the game and scrum-halves in particular. Joshua shuddered as he looked at the cold fish like eyes and the weak flabby chin of the council chairman. There was more warmth and feeling in a plate of last week's tripe. The meeting droned on, tea was served by the caretaker from a trolley, and at last, at 9.30p.m., the second half of the meeting began.

In black and white it was stated in the agenda for the meeting that proposed aid for Bramfield R.L.F.C. was to be discussed. Joshua cleared his throat. It was muck or nettles now. It could be his finest hour, or was it to be his 'Waterloo'? It was time to show what he was made of. He wouldn't go down without one hell of a fight. For a start, he pulled out a green and yellow muffler from his pocket and draped it around his neck, then a beret of the same colours was placed on his head, and he completed the scenario by producing a large rattle from a Co-op carrier bag. He was in his Wembley attire. He had last been similarly dressed when the lads had came home victorious from the twin towers in 1931. Jeremiah Crumpsall sneered.

"What's this Joshua? Are you giving us a turn? You'll be on Hippodrome next with Two-Ton Tessie O'Shea. You'd make a good pair cavorting on stage and a good second row for Rovers an all!"

Jeremiah's jest caused a great laugh. The Rovers man ignored it and rose to his full height. He looked bizarre but impressive. This was his chance to show his oratory off to its full powers. He felt quite shakespearian. He began:

"I come here to bury Rovers, not to praise them! Nay, nay, not quite to bury them, we hope, (I speak metabollically) but to save them from the grave. That is more correct, gentlemen, and I stand here tonight as chairman of your rugby league football club to appeal to this council for help to save the club from death. It is staring the club in the face. It's cadaverous features are upon the Rovers, and its cold lifeless hands are pointing to their demise."

"Joshua must have etten a dictionary for his tea." remarked Councillor Gormley.

The Rovers man paused for a few second to let the weighty words sink in. That was enough of the classics, he'd get down to brass tacks now. Talk plain.

"Bramfield Rugby League club was formed in 1912 by a local man, William Glover, who played for the team for a few seasons. He was an amateur, a fine young man who believed in sport and recreation for the masses. A man who encouraged youth of the town to indulge in open air activities in order to counteract the conditions they worked in down the mine and in the factory. He also realised that a rugby club could bring great joy to people, put the town on the map, bring great light and relief into their miserable lives. Bramfield was then and still is a

34

depressed town, as we are all aware. To go the match on Saturday has been the only joy in many folks' dull lives. Rovers' have brought hope and happiness into a town that badly needs it."

"Ere ere." piped up Councillor Heneberry, who had been allowed back into the chamber. Joshua gave him a smile of thanks then continued. "Ask any spectator and he'll tell you that t'Rovers mean the world to him - aye, and women too. It's a family club, is Rovers. Town are proud of them, gentlemen, even though we are down in the dumps both in the playing and financial sense....."

"We're all aware of that, Councillor," interrupted Jeremiah. "and we haven't got all neet." he added.

"In 1926 we won Lancashire Cup, 1928 we won Lancashire League, and in 1930 we got to the final of the championship, losing by one point to the mighty Salford.. ...."

"I've asked thee to get on with it, Councillor!" barked Jeremiah. Joshua realised that he had committed a faux-pas. Mentioning Salford, of all teams, in front of old Crumpsall, he wanted stringing up from the goal posts for committing such an error.

"I'm trying to establish a picture for the council members of a very important aspect of life in our town. It is essential that I remind them of our successes.....now.....aye....where was I? That's right .....It were in 1929 that we beat Australia by ten points to seven and them with the mighty Armbuster in the forrards and Gorman and Finch in the backs. He were a flyer were Finch, but he never got over Rovers' line that day. Little Davey King, still black from the pit, where he had just done a shift, marked him like a good 'un. Tackled him into ground. It were a proud day for the town, beating Australia. That was the spirit of Bramfield, the Aussies thought Davey was a blackman, he were so dirty. They couldn't believe their eyes when they saw him afterwards at the reception. He were injured in a pit accident, were Davey, and he's only got one arm now. His only pastime is watching Rovers on a Saturday. Closure of club would break his heart, as it would thousands of other folk in Bramfield. Decent, God-fearing folk who live for honest to goodness sport, rate-payers who support our little town. Men and women of Bramfield who have carried the banner of Bramfield on hunger marches before now. The salt of the earth. You're own kind, gentlemen. You're very own. Will you let them down? Nay, nay, surely you would never do that....nay!"

"He'll be bringing his violin out next." said Jeremiah to the treasurer.

"He hasn't got guts to do that." chirped up Albert Heneberry. Jeremiah turned on him with a ferocious snarl.

"I'm sick of thy jokes, Councillor, heartsick of them! You're more suited to Hippodrome than council chamber".

At this juncture, Councillor Farrell rose to his feet.

"Mr Hepplethwaite - I address you as Mr. because you are now representing Bramfield R.L.F.C. What went wrong at the club? Tell us that. Why are you in such a mess?"

"Through the chair, if you please, Councillor Farrell." barked Jeremiah, who was a stickler for council etiquette and decorum.

"I'll leave it at that Mr Chairman. I want to repeat, through the chair, what went wrong at the club, Councillor Hepplethwaite?"

"If you'll let me finish, I'll tell thee." Joshua was sweating profusely now and his bladder was threatening to burst.

"Although we won glory at Wembley in 1933 we lost money. Because most of our speccies couldn't travel due to shortage of funds, the gate wasn't a big one, smallest ever. Hotel costs were astronomical. Hangers on, who never supported club normally, came to the celebration dinner in London. Folk who have big business in this area of Lancashire suddenly became supporters when Rovers won the cup, and ended up supping all the booze when we had our do on coming home victorious. We can do without fair weather friends, and as you all know gentlemen, this council put on a spread for the players and officials, not to mention yourselves, and then sent bill to me as chairman of t'club...aye, you're own club, that had won the Rugby League Cup. You wouldn't even stand that out of council funds. We put the town on the sporting map and you couldn't even treat us to a meal."

"It was you're idea to have a spread if we won." pointed out Councillor Farrell, who owned the Hippodrome but secretly hated the Rovers because he reckoned they drained folk of money they could have spent at his theatre.

"Aye, I agree Councillor Farrell, but not to pay for it. Then we had injuries one after another. Two players had to pack up, big Harry Challoner was suspended sine die for kicking referee at Batley. He needed kicking an all. Harry's crime were that he was caught doing it.

36

If he'd been a Wigan player, I don't doubt ref would have turned a blind eye. The welsh connection dried up, local talent seemed to vanish then Leeds bought two of best welshmen and Hull another, then we had a fire in committee room and that cost a fortune because insurance wouldn't pay out, because thay said it was caused by a director's cigar....we fought 'em and lost, and that cost more money. That were three year ago, and things have gone downhill since. We had a run of thirteen matches without a win, and finished bottom but one, and ever since we've been at the bottom. Ground's in a mess. League's said that some teams have complained about player's facilities. All in all, we're up creek and no paddle. In a word, bankrupt."

Joshua sat down.

"How much?" It was a blunt question from Jerimiah.

The reply was equally blunt. "2,000 quid, Mr Chairman."

"If you will leave the room, we will vote on it."

Joshua was almost glad. His sphincter was leaking.

When he returned after five minutes, it was to a room full of chatter. But what sort of chatter was it? He could tell it certainly wasn't about the Rovers. He stood by the doorway to listen. That old bugger Farrell's on about his theatre, thought Joshua, and he was right.

"Next week we've got a belting bill," he was telling his pals.

"Nat Mills and Bobby. Cavan O'Connor 'The Strolling Vagabond'. Fred Stretch, 'The India rubber Man', and Musical Dawson's Canaries, an extravaganza of bird song."

"Can we get in cheep, Councillor Farrell? Do you get it? Cheep....ee, no sense of ruddy humour." It was Albert Heneberrry trying to be funny again. Joshua ignored the banter and sat down, embarassed coughing had started up again. Joshua knew he was defeated. The secretary rose to his feet.

"I will now announce, gentlemen, the result of the ballot. There were four votes in favour of helping Bramfield R.L.F.C. financially and ten against."

Joshua raised his fist and shook it at Jeremiah Crumpsall.

"Judas!" he thundered. "How dare you turn your backs on the town team in their hour of need? Shame on the lot of you!"

"It was a fair vote, Councillor." replied the chairman.

"Fair me backside, they're a lily livered lot on this council. Frightened

37

of offending you. Well, I'll tell you to your face, Jeremiah. You're an old skin flint with no civic pride and no back bone......All you want is your own glory. I'll get this put in the papers, mark my word, and I hope speccies lynch you. This council's as much concern for Rovers as an incontinent pigeon has for an open air sports meeting. And you're a flaming hypocrite an all, to boot....does Barrow ring a bell, Mr Chairman.... the Bridge Hotel, to be precise?"

Councillor Crumpsall turned three shades of grey. "B...Barrow? Should it?"

"You know what I mean. I were fog bound one neet in Barrow after I'd been doing a spot of scouting at an A team match so I had to stop over at Bridge Hotel and I saw thee and thee weren't alone. Nice piece she were 'an all."

"I were on holiday in Lakes with Men's Fellowship....what's it got to with you, anyroads up?"

"Nowt, Jeremiah, nowt, but I'm sick of being a member of a council what's run by a whited sep-ulchre."

He liked that phrase so much he repeated it with relish. "A whited sep-ulchre, that's what you are. And that's in Bible, no less."

"I've got power to expel thee." ranted Jeremiah. "Did you hear him? get thee mouth washed out, Councillor!"

"I will, at Crown, over t'road. It'll take a few pints to wash away the smell of you bunch of traitors. I'll be sending in my official resignation, Mr Secretary."

"Aye, and it'll be accepted, an all. We don't want your sort on this council!" spat Jeremiah.

"Shut up! Thar's all man and shirt." taunted the rugby league man. They faced each other like two angry dogs over a bone. Jeremiah like a ruptured whippet, and Joshua like an injured bulldog.

"It would be different if it were Farrell's theatre, wouldn't it?" Joshua spoke slowly, with great deliberation.

"What does mean by that?....Explain yourself." said the theatre owner.

"Why, it's common knowledge when Nugent's Naughty Nudes were booked to come to Hippodrome, all churches were up in arms, but council did'nt stop 'em coming, did they?...Nay, it were fixed between you two. Common knowledge. I'll scratch your back and you scratch

38

mine."

Joshua pointed to the two men he was accusing.

"Back handers, perks, that's what you and your spleen on t'council are after, Jeremiah... Rovers have never been a fashionable club, so you've never been in favour because they couldn't feather your nest. Never do owt for nowt, that's your motto. You'd make a good Yorkshireman!"

"I'll sue thee, Joshua Hepplewhaite!"

Farrell, the theatre owner was deadly serious as he pointed a fat finger at the rugby man. Joshua blew a wet raspberry, gave them the V sign, and left the room.

The row had shocked the council chamber. Jeremiah and Councillor Farrell were acutely embarrassed by what Joshua had said. There was a deep silence for several minutes, broken only by the secretary who spoke in whispers about the next meeting to several members. And then shouting and singing broke out on the street below. Joshua stood on the pavement waving his rattle furiously. "Up Rovers!" He was ranting. "And up thee an all, Jeremiah. May God forgive you, Rovers' speccies never will!"

He was in time for last orders at the Crown. The landlord was so upset by the bad news that he closed the doors and allowed after hours drinking. The pub was the unofficial headquarters of the supporters' club. The news was met with disbelief. The supporters had never really believed that the club would close. One man suggested beating up Jeremiah Crumpsall and hanging him by his braces from the popular stand, but Jeremiah persuaded his hostile followers to seek solace in another pint of Bradshaw's best mild instead.

Gradually the crowd dispersed and went home, full of mild beer and sadness. Joshua threw caution over his complaint to the wind, and set about getting pie-eyed with the landlord of the Crown. Eventually, at 5 .o'clock the next morning, he managed to flag down a plasterer making an early start, and begged a lift on his hand cart. As the cart was trundled along the cobbles of Gaswork Street the disgusted face of Acid Alice peeped through the net curtains of number 22. Joshua was yelling, "Up Rovers!" with gusto. From the corner of his eye the plasterer could see the figure of a burly man in blue bearing down upon them. He began to run like hell over the cobbles, bumping his passenger up and down, like a sizzling sausage on a red hot pan. The law caught up with them at the bottom of the street.

"Well, I'll go t'foot of our stairs, it's thee, Mr Hepplethwaite."

"Aye lad, it's me, who did you expect, the Agar Khan?" asked a much sober Joshua. "And I've got some news for thee an all. Rovers have got to finish, no more brass, I were at council meeting last night, and they refused to help us. Lock me up if it will do any good, lad, I couldn't give a damn, anyroads up."

P.C. Fred Bland had played for the Rovers as a hooker in the late twenties. He was stunned by what Joshua had told him, but Fred was no fool. Police duty was police duty. He had to be seen to be doing his duty as well. This street wasn't known as the street of the 'squinting windows' for nothing. He was aware of many pairs of eyes watching him. He spoke in a loud voice. "I'll have to summon thee, and thee Mr Jones, for aiding and abetting this breach of the peace. There'll be no knockers-up needed this morning. You've woken street up with your goings on."

Several residents were making their way towards them, and had heard what the constable had said. P.C. Bland scribbled diligently in his little notebook.

"I should think so, an all." said Acid Alice, who was wearing a coat that looked as if it had seen service in the Crimea. Thus appeased, the residents dispersed.

Joshua gave the P.C. a cold look. "Et tu, Bruti?" He was trying his hand at Shakespeare again. The constable did not answer until the cart had been wheeled around the corner.

He answered in actions, tearing up the page in his notebook he pointed to Marsh's field with his thumb. "Beat it, before I change me mind, the pair of thee!"

The relieved plasterer did as he was bidden at the double. P.C. Bland wiped a tear from his eye and slowly turned back up Gasworks Street for an early morning cup of tea at the bakehouse, proud in the knowledge that he had done his duty. He knew he was known locally as a bit of a bastard but, nay, he wasn't that bad.

Chapter 4

Introducing Clarence Sneem

Clarence Sneem was sitting in the editorial office of the Bramfield Trumpet listening to his new electric horn gramophone. Such machines were almost unknown in Lancashire, being bespoke models purchased by music lovers of the wealthier classes. Clarence was such a snob that he considered that it was the right thing for him to posses one. After all, he was the editor of the newspaper. The huge paper mache horn was blaring out in stentorian tones: Ocean, Thy Mighty Monster, from the opera Oberon, by Weber. He had no idea what the song was all about, but he liked to feel that he had intellectual pursuits, even though he had been brought up on the popular songs of such artists as George Formby Senior and Billy Williams, 'The man in the velvet suit'. But when you were in his position and rubbing shoulders with such influential people as mill owners and colliery bosses, one had to disguise one's working class roots. If a newspaper had set up deliberately calling itself the 'Gutter Press', he would have been the automatic choice as editor. Most of the Bramfield folk disliked him for they knew he was 'peas above sticks', an old Lancashire saying which meant that he was a snob.

Clarence was a ruthless wielder of the pen, and had little regard for people's feelings and reputations. Commonly known as a crawler and a creep by the old folk who knew his parents, he was unashamedly sycophantic when he thought that the interests of his newspaper could be furthered by 'sucking up' to people of affluence, particularly those cotton 'kings' who made their money out of cheap labour in the shabby towns and left each night to return to their palatial homes in the pleasant

41

and green suburbs of Manchester and the borders of Cheshire. He tried his best to forget that his father had been a 'lasher-on' in the pit and had no pride in the fact that he was remembered as the best wicket keeper in West Lancashire. 'Stumper Sneem', as his dad had been known to his mates, was said to have been good enough to have played for the county, but he was not prepared to relinquish his job for the uncertainty of a sporting career. The story was still told in the town, much to Clarence's embarrassment, of how his father had whitewashed his pit boots in order to play when his cricket boots were consigned to the midden.

Clarence himself was no stranger to poverty, even though he had tried to erase the memory of his early days. He hated meeting those old school pals who would remind him gleefully of when they played for the 'Raggy Arse Rangers', who used a local cinder field. He always strongly denied that in his infancy he had been helped by the Clog and Stocking fund.

He took the record off the turn-table, and was about to replace it with 'O Rest In The Lord' from Elijah, by Mendelssohn, an aria he often sang in the choir on a Sunday morning, when there was a knock on the door. "Mr Hepplethwaite to see you, Mr Sneem." sang out his secretary. Clarence had been expecting him. He was well aware of what had happened at the council meeting the night before. Jeremiah Crumpsall, a personal friend, had told him all about it as soon as the office opened. In any case, he had known all along that the council had no desire to help the local rugby league team. He rose, and held out a flabby hand to the chairman, who took it with little enthusiasm. Joshua had no time for Clarence, and the feeling was mutual. They greeted each other politely.

"I'll come to the point, Mr Sneem." said Joshua. "I want you to let your readers know that the town team has been stabbed in the back by the council. I called the chairman, Mr Crumpsall, a Judas to his face, and that's what he is. You can print that."

He then proceeded to tell the editor the story which he took down in shorthand,

"I'm relying on you, Mr Sneem, for I want t'folks of Bramfield to know the truth. Appen you'll hear different stories from other folks on t'council. I may be a blunt sort of fella, but I am honest. Good morning

42

to you." They exchanged handshakes and the interview was at an end.

Sneem put a Clara Butt record on the turn-table and made a few notes for the article which was to go in the weekend edition of the Trumpet. Joshua was an old windbag but over the years the Rovers had been good copy for his newspaper. He had often gone to matches himself to write reports and had met many influential journalists who had helped him to syndicate nationally news he had gathered locally. However, he did not want to offend Jeremiah Crumpsall, who had been a good friend to the newspaper in exchange for some exaggerated reportage about his good work and charitable deeds in the town. Clarence knew that it didn't pay to openly fall out with anyone and that the ideal way was to 'run with the fox and hunt with the hounds'.

He locked his office door and took a small key from his waist coat pocket with which he opened a cabinet. This was his private hiding hole for snippets of news and juicy scandal which could be used when the opportunity presented itself. No-one else knew about it. "Now where is it?" he said to himself as he rummaged furiously through the documents and papers. "Here it is, the very thing! I think we can use this very shortly. Soon the time will be ripe." Clarence smirked in the knowledge that he could make a killing from the notes he had just perused.

At breakfast time on the Friday morning, Joshua eagerly picked up the local paper from the hall. The front page bore headlines of local interest, but there was no mention of the Rovers. He found a couple of columns about the club on page three.

'Council Regret No Help For Rovers'

At the Town Council meeting on Monday night, the financial plight of Bramfield Rovers was given a sympathetic hearing. 'We had to turn them down, it was a hard decision for the Committee to make.' Jeremiah Crumpsall, the council Chairman told a Trumpet correspondent. 'There are so many improvements needed in the town, that we haven't the financial resources available. We intend to improve facilities in the town, and a new lavatory will be constructed in Fletcher

Park. The lake will also be re-stocked with fish.' he informed our correspondent.

'Councillor Hepplethwaite put a very strong case forward to the Council on behalf of the rugby league club. A vote was taken which went against the Rovers, although regrets were offered by council members who felt that the people of Bramfield's welfare came first.' Councillor Hepplethwaite said 'The Rovers are still carrying on, we hope the folk of Bramfield will support us in our darkest hour. We will definitely be fielding a team at St.Helens Recs. on Saturday.'

Joshua read it silently, then handed it to his wife to read. He was not surprised. Clarence Sneem was a master of invention and now that the club was on its 'uppers', he had no more interest in them. He finished his cup of tea and remarked "It's coming to summat when a piss-oile is more important than the town team. Second fiddle to a urinal, it beats bloody band does that!"

Chapter 5

An Emergency Meeting

Joshua let himself into the ground through a rickety gate which badly needed new hinges. It was a cold, clear moonlit night with a distinct hint of hoar frost in the air. As he trudged over the crisp cinders towards the pavilion he felt an eeriness which was difficult to ignore. The pitch was illuminated by the moonlight and aided and abetted by a pair of flickering victorian gas lamps standing in a street nearby. It was a perfect evening for ghosts. The sight of the pitch lured him to the old fence upon which tens of thousands of spectators had leaned over the years – as he gazed at the arena he could see figures of the past, – – – – spectators swarming to congratulate the team after the great victory over Australia, ... Albert Wagstaffe the great Huddersfield centre striding majestically down the middle. . . . . . .

As the phantom brigade passed before his eyes Joshua shook his head and laughed to himself at how susceptible the mind can be to suggestions and to situations. He had never felt like this before and yet he felt happy and at ease with these visions of the past. The old ground was part of his very being and he was part of it. The Hepplethwaites had always been Rovers people, he could recall helping his dad light the braziers which were used to soften frosty ground and even carried a scar on his leg through getting accidentally stabbed by a pitch fork when men were covering the field with straw. He could still feel the dig of the doctors needle in the casualty department but even in pain he had turned up to watch the lads in a cup tie.

The Rovers' ground was known as Marl Heights, set in an elevated part

45

of the town, and by virtue of this exposed position regularly buffeted by winds and the excesses of wintry weather. Even when the club had its share of glory back in 1931 with the great Wembley victory and a high place in the league, the ground was never one of the smartest venues in the game. The directors had planned to do a lot of repairs, and to make structural alterations to grandstands and terraces. Despite the Wembley success, the bank balance was not healthy enough to undertake the improvements, and with the massive unemployment problem, and the team's loss of form, the jobs were never done. Gales had ripped holes in the stand. One part of the terracing had been closed when huge gaps had appeared. The old fence surrounding the pitch was rickety and unsafe, and the timbering of the stands and the pavilion was in a deplorable state due to a lack of paint. Flooding was a regular feature due to intensive repairs needed to the drainage system. This state of disrepair extended to the pavilion with almost spartan conditions prevailing for the players in the changing rooms. Even the old speaking tube used by the directors to summon the players to the board room was hanging limp and useless next to a huge crack in the plaster in the players' refreshment room. The whole aspect was a sad and sorry one, and yet many rugby league clubs had similar problems at this period. While most struggled on, keeping their heads above water, Bramfield Rovers were on the verge of being drowned in a sea of debt and financial embarrassment

Joshua found his co-directors waiting for him in the board room. The Kearsley Brothers, Bert and Bob, were bachelors who would have died rather than see their beloved team go to the knacker's yard. They were the proprietors of a building firm founded by their father, a noted martinet who had made the lads work on saturdays and school holidays when their pals were enjoying themselves. Rather than stifle their interest in sport, this rough treatment had only served to make them 'mustard' keen on the Rovers. They sneaked off work whenever the opportunity arose to watch their heroes play. When the business became their own, they indulged their new-found freedom and affluence to the full, and bought themselves onto the Rovers' board. It was common knowledge that they had tried to ease the financial state of the club from their own pockets. As bachelors they were more able to do this, than had they been married with dependant families: but enough

'HAVE A PICKLE YOUR LORDSHIP'

(A scene from Rover's past glory days)

was enough, they could only to do so much. No one appreciated this more than Joshua. The three men were great pals, and the camaraderie at the club had been renowned throughout the league.

"Well Gentlemen, the vultures are gathering" announced Joshua as they sat together in the boardroom. "I went to the bank today. They are adamant. The shop's shut. No brass."

"Have a pickle." said Bob Kearsley, handing his jar around. He was known to the directors of other clubs as 'Pickle Kearsley', and had taken a bottle into the best stand at Wembley, and even offered one to Lord Derby. Between chews, he explained that their building business was going through a bad time, and they couldn't put any more money into the club.

"By rights, we should be laying men off, but we haven't got the heart to do it." he told them.

Joshua knew it was the truth and said. "We've all tried, but it seems we're beat. We've had us ups and down, but this time poverty's got us by its icy tentacles, and the death knell is booming in the stygian darkness of our private hell on earth."

Bert laughed "By the heck, he's been at the metal polish again! He should have been one of them damp - attic actors. Hee hee hee that's what me dad used to call 'em. He hadn't much fun in him, me dad, but he did like to mess about with words..... what's wrong with thee, our Bob? You've got a face on you like a wet day at Wilderspool."

"Since the secretary gave his notice in - not that I blame him, like, seeing we couldn't afford to pay him - I've got all the paper work to do and it's not my favourite sort of thing, and I'm worried sick about how we're going to afford trip to Hull for first round of the cup. Three matches away on the run, and no brass coming through the turnstiles. Ain't it amazing how bad luck follows upon bad luck? I reckon we should go on the train to Hull, it's better for the players, and I don't reckon as it's a good idea to use cars, it's too far, is Hull. I met our winger, Dodger Dean, in the market today, and he says, he won't travel in Stanley Keighley's hearse again. It made him feel sick, and he had to get out twice on the way to St.Helens. I know we have to cut our cloth, so to speak, but I think it's a bit morbid sending the players in a funeral limousine, Joshua." The chairman gave a half nod of his head.

"I wish we were at home, we've had some good hidings in Yorkshire and I don't relish another. I'm fair fed up with that road over the moors. 'From Hull, Hell, and Halifax may the good Lord deliver us'. By gum it's proving a true saying for the Rovers. I don't see owt wrong in a funeral car if it's nice and comfy. We can't afford to be choosy tha knows." Joshua stuck his jaw out defiantly.

"I agree with brother Bob, it is a bit macabre." said Bert. "Besides, I don't think the lads can give of their best in such circumstances."

"You not blaming defeat at Recs. on some of them travelling in a hearse, surely Bert? We did lose 42 points to six. Are you suggesting we'd have beat 'em if we'd gone first class on the train?"

"There's no need for sarcasm, Joshua." said Bert.

Joshua gave Bert a good natured dig in the ribs.

"Nay Bert, I don't mean it, I agree, it's not a nice way to travel. Yes, I think we should go to Hull on the train."

"I second that, but what do we use for money, scotch mist?" asked Bob, helping himself to a pickle. At this juncture, Joshua placed his thumbs behind his braces and expanded his chest, then removed a gold watch from the fob pocket of his waistcoat and announced:

"I have the answer, gentlemen. I have been offered a very handsome price for this watch. Very handsome indeed, and I'm taking it. It'll just about cover the cost of a trip to Hull."

"But it's your pride and joy, Joshua lad! We can't allow you to do that. You were always so proud of that watch." said Bob.

"Rightly so, lad." agreed Joshua.

"I won it brass-banding in Yorkshire, competing against blokes from Black Dyke and Brighouse and Rastrick. They're the Leeds and Huddersfields of the brass band world, but I beat 'em on their own middens. I could fair make a cornet talk in those days, but I've no puff left now..... no, I insist it goes."

"Well, what can we say, except that it's a reet noble gesture on your part, Josh. And I think thee deserves another pickle. Well, I suppose you want to know how me and Bert went on at Blackpool yesterday?"

"I gathered you didn't have any success, Bob, or you would have mentioned it earlier. Did they lend a sympathetic ear?"

"Oh aye. Me and Bob told the Mayor how the miners and mill workers of Bramfield had poured thousands of pounds into Blackpool. After all, Blackpool has always been the favourite recreation place for northern

'WHEERS THE BLOODY CHIPS?'

working folk. Our Bert told him how in Wakes Week the railway station was packed solid. It was a regular sight to see a half-mile queue and police brought in to control them. Then we told him the stark truth about the club."

"Was he impressed?" asked Joshua.

"Oh aye, but it seems Blackpool's skint an all, they're going through a bad time due to the slump. They'd have liked to have helped us of course, but they weren't in a position to do so. He were a nice gentlemen, but blunt. He gave us a knife and fork tea in the parlour instead....tinned salmon and cucumber and a pint of ale at Uncle Tom's Cabin on the way to the station."

"Always come away with summat, that's my motto. You did your best lads. The good Lord loves a trier."

Joshua blew heartily into his polka dot handkerchief as if to emphasise his remark.

Bob Kearsley tried to dispel the gloom.

"Let's not dwell upon doom and woe, we've got plenty of happy memories. Besides, I've always had a belief that God moves in mysterious ways. Appen a miracle might occur. I've always read the good book, and there's lots of examples of how God turned the tide of disaster for many folk."

Joshua nodded his head.

"Appen so, Bob, but I don't think as it mentions rugby league clubs in the good book. I'm not being facetious, but I reckon you're clutching at straws like the proverbial drowning man. Still, you're right when you mention happy times. I'll never forget when the club ladies used to make butties up when we couldn't afford to stop on long journeys. We had many a picnic."

"Aye, and we never thought it would happen again." said Bob, bringing his chairman back to reality.

"Albert Heneberry and his Supporters' Committee have been real bricks, I went over to see him and he's arranged for his members to help out. They'll man the turnstiles and sell programmes and some of them have offered to help the groundsman clean up the terraces. Them's the sort of good-hearted folk owd Crumpsall and his cronies are turning their backs on." added Bob.

"Aye, we've still got some good friends." said Joshua. "We thought we were badly done to back in the twenties, but it's far worse this time. What about when Lionel Cook the baker helped us out with the team jerseys? He had his flour bags made up for us by a bespoke tailor in Cheetham Hill."

It was Bert's turn to reminisce now.

"What about that time we gave the lads a treat and took them to that posh hotel in Windermere for a five course dinner on the way home from that cup victory at Barrow? Do you remember 'Crusher Casey' from over Widnes way? He hadn't been around much hadn't 'Crusher', and when he saw the fish course, he wondered what he was getting. It was a small piece of grilled haddock in parsley sauce. He yelled out, "Wheer's the bloody chips?" at the top of his voice.

Bob had opened the committee drinks cabinet and was pouring out generous fingers of spirit. They were warming to their memories. It was Joshua's turn to wind back the clock of nostalgia.

"What about little Archie Gummerstonethwaite we got on loan from Liverpool Stanley? He couldn't spell, so he comes up to me one day and says "How do you spell wattle, Mr Chairman?" He was writing a letter home. "I want me mam to send me a tie for the club christmas do", he says. So I says to him "Give me the sentence, then I'll try and help you." He pulls out the letter and reads "Dear mam, please send me a tie wattle go with me new club blazer."

It was pickles and whisky all round, and anyone passing the club house would have been forgiven for thinking that the directors were having a party. Like men condemned to die, they were enjoying one last night of fun.

Chapter Six

Sneem Plays Dirty

Clarence Sneem had reported the match at Hull. Another debacle, the first leg of the first round of the Challenge Cup. Beaten by 37 points to 6, the Rovers had the prospect before them of another good hiding on their own ground when the second leg was played. They were fast becoming a joke, the daily papers were making good copy out of the fact that they had now broken the record for the longest number of consecutive defeats. The wily editor sensed that the time was right. On the Sunday night after the Hull game, he attended a charity concert promoted by the League Of Help, sitting in a box alongside members of the clergy and civic dignitaries. He liked to be seen to be doing good. The concert was given by Tom Burke, [5] the great tenor, who had once been a coal miner in Leigh. His working class roots appealed to northern people, and his concerts were always a sell-out. After the recital, Mr Sneem interviewed the tenor for his newspaper, then took supper with Jeremiah Crumpsall at the councillor's house.

Afterwards he walked quietly along the gas lit streets to his office. He was like a thief slinking through the darkness, and his motives were hardly more honourable. After warming himself against the frosty air with a large scotch, he took out the secret batch of papers from a cabinet. As he sat back to peruse them, his mind drifted back to that evening two years before when he had met Stanley Keighley after an evening match. The scout was hardly his sort of person, but he tolerated his company on this occasion, for he knew it was his opportunity to milk him for the story about the alleged signing of a man with a wooden leg. He knew that Stanley was putty in his hands if he got the whisky bottle out. 'Just a quick one' in the editorial office resulted in several more until Stanley's reserves had dropped and he was a man willing to expose all his secrets, particularly his private life and his wife's coldness towards him. He was a man unloved, a man given to bouts of drinking to mask his unhappiness. Clarence pretended to listen to the litany with sympathy and gradually changed the subject round to that fateful trip to Wales. Stanley, unsuspectingly, told him exactly what had occurred.

Clarence poured himself another drink as he thought of the angle he would adopt for the story. He knew that the scout's tale was an incredible one, but hardly sensational. It needed spicing up. He could provide the sauce. The joke element was all very well, but as a story it would only be average, especially for the Sunday papers, unless it was liberally laced with hyperbole. With a satisfied grin on his face, he settled himself at his old Remington, and typed out the following story for syndication.

SAGA OF A DRUNKEN RUGBY SCOUT AND A CHEATING LEAGUE CLUB

The dreadful plight of Bramfield Rovers rugby league team is a major talking point for sports journalists, and all who are concerned with rugby league. Are they close to being a defunct club? The team with the dubious honour of holding the record for the number of consecutive defeats, has always been noted for its 'rum' characters, both on the field and in the boardroom, but there has been none 'rummer' than Stanley Keighley, a local undertaker. Mr Keighley openly admits that he 'likes a drink' to counteract his wife's lack of affection. He also owns up to several faux pas during his duties as chief scout for the Rovers. His most celebrated blunder was committed in Neath Rugby Union Club about five years ago. After watching a match between Neath and Cross Keys, he was disappointed that the player he had in mind had performed poorly. Assuming that no-one knew who he was, he went for a drink in the club bar. His reputation as something of a 'boyo', especially after a few pints, was well known by the union fraternity of the valleys. He was soon recognised by two Cross Keys players who

'HELLO AGAIN BOYO........
I'M YOUR NEW HOOKER FROM THE VALLEYS'

had stayed on for a drinking session. They decided to play a trick on him. A friend of theirs 'Peg Leg' Dai Owen, was also in the bar. Dai had been a hooker for Neath until he had lost a leg in a colliery railway accident. He was noted for practical jokes and gambling. If there was a bet going, he could never refuse a flutter, no matter how crazy it was. The players told Dai that he could make himself some money, but first he must go home and find a pair of trousers which would disguise his deformity. By the time he returned, the northern scout was on his fourth beer with a whisky chaser. The two Cross Keys men then approached him and told him they could recommend a very fine hooker who was keen to turn professional. Mr Keighley immediately pricked up his ears, the Rovers were short of a good hooker, and soon he was in deep conversation with Dai Owen who praised his own ability as a procurer of the ball from the scrum. Forty pounds as a retainer was handed over in cash and the rest of the night was spent in drinking and singing ribald rugby songs. Mr Keighley joined in the fun with gusto, removing his pants and singing 'My Brudder Sylveste', clad only in his long johns and a Rovers scarf.

'Peg Leg' Owen thought the incident was finished, but the next day the two players bet him ten pounds that he wouldn't travel to Bramfield to meet the directors, and promised him free drink for a month if he did. The scout was informed of the new player's travelling arrangements, and he made an appointment to meet him at Bramfield station on the following Wednesday. We can only leave it to the reader's imagination. Picture the scene: a man with a wooden stump for a leg is standing on the platform greeting the representative of his new club. "Good morning, Mr Keighley, remember me, I'm the new hooker." It could not have been bettered in a Will Hay comedy.

Although furious at the deception, and humiliated by his own stupidity, the scout, being a true tight northerner, decided he would have his money's worth. He explained the faux pas to the Rovers' committee, Messrs. Hepplethwaite and Bob and Bert Kearsley. The Welshman told them he could still hook, despite his infirmity. When he had unfolded his secret plan, he was put straight into the Rover's first team. Before the match, Bramfield's trainer inserted a magnet inside the match ball. The hooker turned out in white trousers, with his stump sunk into a specially prepared boot which had a strip of metal attached to it. As a *player in the loose he was no use, but in the scrum he won every ball, giving the Rovers' three quarters a day to remember, and a fine victory for the team. This contravention of league rules was never discovered, but the directors were frightened that the deception could not last, especially playing away from home. They paid him for his trouble and put him on the train back to the valleys. It is hardly surprising that such a club are in dire straits.*

Clarence read over his destructive piece of journalism, and was well pleased with the work. After another whisky, he rang up for a taxi to take him home, not caring a jot for the hurt the article would cause.

Chapter Seven

The Scandal Breaks

The second leg of the first round of the Rugby League Cup had been played against Hull at Marl Heights with the Bramfield lads once again being targeted as the rubbing rags of the league. Stanley Keighley was soaking in a zinc bath tub in front of the parlour fire. It was Monday morning. As Stanley added a liberal fist full of mustard to the water from the Colman's tin he contemplated the good hiding his team had received at the hands of the lads from Craven Park. The spirit had gone out of the players. They were like donkeys who had made too many journeys and had taken too many floggings. New blood was needed badly but was out of the question. Local talent had dried up and those lads who were showing promise were going to the richer, more successful clubs. To add to Stanleys misery he was aching all over. That dilapidated grandstand full of holes with gaps in the roof that let in snow, had caused him to get a bad chill. Even a flask of piping hot cocoa liberally laced with rum ('not a word to Clara think on!') had failed to warm him up. He remembered how Joshua Hepplethwaite always got the whisky bottle out after a match but this luxury had gone by the board. Frozen to the marrow he had spent Sunday in bed. The fire was roaring in the grate as he soaked his sore limbs in the hot soapy water. He always enjoyed a Monday morning. Clara got up early to go to her mother's to do the Monday wash. He could enjoy himself with her out of the way, and if he slopped the water all over the linoleum so what? There was plenty of time for him to mop it up. There was no one to bury this morning so he could enjoy an extra long soak. Normally he would have been in a contented mood, even though the Rover's had lost. He

58

was used to defeats – – – no, it went deeper than that. He was down in the dumps because he knew in his heart that he would soon lose a part of his life – – – his beloved rugby team. They just couldn't carry on the way things were going.

Ever since being knee-high to a corner flag he had supported the local team. His dad, Moses Keighley, had been a gateman at Marl Heights in those early pioneer days when the club had for its chairman 'Trust in the Lord' Arkwright, a hell fire lay preacher who was mad on Rugby League.

After a home victory it was the practice of old Arkwright to gather all the club officials and players together for prayers and hymn singing. Stanley could remember being lifted on his father's shoulders to watch Albert Rosenfeld the flying Huddersfield winger, scoring a try against Rovers. And would he ever forget dashing onto the pitch to get the autograph of Charlie Seeling, the great Kiwi forward who played for Wigan? Like any other supporter he had experienced the vagaries of being a fan, the elation and the heartbreak, but a long series of defeats can deject even the most ardent follower of a club. Failure breeds despair. The latest defeats had been especially demoralising and humiliating. After a greatly improved display at home to Batley, when they went down by only a couple of points, they had slipped to that devastating reverse at Rochdale, followed by drubbings at St Helens Recs, Hull home and away, and a mid-week thrashing away to Barrow. They had reached the abyss, the lowest ebb, a lane without a turning. Not only would he lose his job as chief scout for the club he would lose part of his very existence. Rugby wasn't just a hobby like ferret breeding, pigeon racing, and whist drives, it was a passion. Life could never be the same for him again. Just like the bubbles that rose from the bath to burst in the heat of the parlour, his dreams had been shattered. His whole life was the Rovers. Everything else was secondary. It was hard to imagine life without rugby league in it.

There was always Clara of course. Their's had never been a steamy, tempestuous relationship, more like a damp bonfire, but he loved her in a funny sort of way. Even though she went to bed with curlers in her hair and kept her khaki stockings on. You have to accept some things in life, he mused – – – – the devil you know and all that – – – and although he fancied Tallulah Bankhead, something rotten, she probably couldn't make taty pie like his Clara. Appen he'd take up hill walking or rambling, they were popular pastimes with northern town dwellers, eager to get the smoke out of their lungs, and it did keep you fit. The more he thought of alternative leisure activities the more morose he became over the Rovers. They would always be his first love – – – aye! Even when defunct. Perhaps he could have done more for the club? Self-doubt began to nag him. He thought of the words of an old song Dai Morgan, the singing prop forward, used to warble at local concerts. "I loved you in life too little, I love you in death too well". Perhaps the words summed up his feelings towards his beloved club. It was a love affair that could never heal.

Some callous acquaintance had remarked that he could travel to watch Wigan, or go to support Salford at Weaste. Only a person with no soul could have uttered such insensitive words. He had no affiliation with any other team – – – aye, that was the very word – – – affiliation – – – he'd be a flaming hypocrite shouting them on at Central Park or Salford. Would a wiganer go to cheer on Saints if the cherry and whites packed in? Would he hell as like! He'd sooner go to the devil first. Could a Leeds die hard possibly feel the same way about Hunslet? No, of course not. Blood is thicker than water. No, he would sooner take up whippet racing or billiards. Even though he'd get an earful from Clara. He gave his back a good rubbing with the soapy loofah and reclined gratefully in the warm soothing water, consoling himself with the thought that things could hardly get worse.

How wrong can a man be? When a man is down and out how often fate can put the rugby boot in with a vengeance.

Clara Keighley was at her mother's. Being a dutiful daughter, she always did the washing for her on a Monday, that traditional day when thousands of northern streets were adorned with washing hanging out to dry. Sheets, underclothes and all manner of garments pegged up on ropes elevated by tall wooden props. The ropes were attached to iron pegs on the houses. Sometimes a whole street would be festooned in this manner, as well as back entries, ginnels, snickets and any available spare land. Clara loved a good wash day, she was in her element at the dolly tub, and was a dab hand with the *dolly pegg.[6] Such christian endeavour made her sing, she'd had a good sing at the chapel the day before. Hymns were her favourite, of course, but she loved the songs of Gracie Fields, the mill girl who had made it big on the music hall and big screen. Clara was an ex-mill girl, so she had a great affection for the Rochdale lass and loved to sing her songs. As she was pegging out in the street, she broke into the 'Rochdale Hounds'. She'd even been told that she sounded like 'Our Gracie', and on this morning was in excellent form, as happy as she had ever been as she sang in full voice:

'I've been hunting with the hounds at Rochdale.
EE by gum! We've got a lovely pack.
Whippets and Alsatians, Bulldogs and Dalmatians.
Horses with two legs in front and two more at the back.
Off we dashed and made a fine display.
Auntie took a fence, and took it with her all the way.
With the Rochdale Hounds at the Rochdale Hunt,
Tally ho! Tally ho!
In hunting dress, instead of clogs and shawls
Jumping over fences and the backyard walls.
Tan tivvy! Tan tivvy! Tan tivvy!
Away, away.....away we went with leaps and bounds.
We couldn't find a fox so with a cat we made pretend.
Uncle Willie rode a horse he'd borrowed from a friend.
Such a lovely thoroughbred, with a coal waggon at the end!
Following the Rochdale hounds.
The horse I rode I borrowed from a circus.
It tried to beg and dance upon its toes.
Father, though he's bandy, he looked fine and dandy.
In a lovely scarlet coat to match his scarlet nose.
Grandpa's horse, it couldn't jump at all.
So all of us, we had to lift it over every wall.
With the Rochdale Hounds, at the Rochdale Hunt.
Tally ho! Tally ho!
In hunting dress instead of clogs and shawls,
jumping over fences and the backyard walls.
Tan tivvy! Tan tivvy! Tan tivvy!
Away, away......away we went with leaps and bounds.
Father's horse flew round the town, and you would hardly
think.
It danced right through the Rose and Crown,

and out in half a wink.
It was the first time Pa had been in a pub and come out
without a drink.
Following the Rochdale Hounds.............'
There are some people in this world who can't stand to see other folks
happy. Ada Dilloway was such a person. Her beady eye was watching
Clara from behind lace curtains. Obviously, Clara didn't know about
the scandal. Being the local busy body and gossip, Ada set out to put
this to rights. Clara's mother, Meg, was steeping her feet in hot water
and mustard in an enamel bowl, a popular northern pastime.

"How long will't dinner be, our Clara?" she sang out through her
faulty dentures.

"A good hour yet, mother. It's lob scouse. Would you like a cup of tea
and a suggestive biscuit? We won't be eating while twelve o'clock."

"Aye, go on lass, i'm fair clemmed."

Clara was mashing the tea when her mother shouted "Someone's
shoved a paper through the letter box, Clara. I didn't order it, did you?"

"No, it must be a good hearted neighbour, i'll get it for you, our mam."

The paper was a treat for the old woman, who scanned the pages
greedily, tut tutting, and whistling through her dentures at the various
tit bits of news. Suddenly she let out an almighty bellow.

"Our Clara, come here!" the old woman's hand shook as she pointed
to an article. "It's about that husband of yours."

"What, my Stanley? Never!"

"Aye, that man you married agin my advice."

"But it can't be about him, not in a daily paper. Appen it's another Mr
Keighley."

"Nay, this one's chief scout for Rovers, and he's an undertaker."

"Well, it *could* be him I suppose." said Clara.

"*Could be*? Of course it's him, you daft beggar!"

"What on earth's he done, mother?" shrieked Clara.

"Done.....done....done? Why, he's sullied his reputation, and yours. I
always said you can never a trust a man who drinks spiritous liquors.
Here, read it yourself lass. We'll be the laughing stock of the town.
Dancing in his long johns with strangers down in Wales. Folk what
can't even speak english proper. You'll be banned from ladies' guild
at St.Wilfreds. Mark my word!"

Clara was scandalised and started to weep. It was an act which annoyed her mother who was made of sterner stuff.

"Stop thee greetin' lass! You're not a child. Sit in the chair yonder and I'll read it to you. You've no gumption in you, our Clara. If I'd have been married to that husband of yours, he'd have been on transfer list long ago, and I wouldn't have wanted a fee for him. He's a drunken philanderer! Scouting for players indeed..... I wonder what else he were scouting for?"

The harsh words caused Clara to burst into tears again. Between sobs she muttered "I knew he were no · Dicky Turner[7] when I married him, but I didn't think he was a boozer.....I am sorry I didn't take any notice of you, mam." The old woman wiped her daughter's eyes with her pinny and hugged her as if she was a child again.

Stanley was busy in his workshop fitting a pair of brass handles to a coffin when he was told about the article by a passing messenger boy who was grinning all over his face. The silence in the corner shop spoke volumes when Stanley went in to buy a paper. With dry lips and shaking hands, he leaned on the bonnet of his hearse and turned over the pages. It was the worst shock he had ever experienced. He broke out in a cold sweat. "I'll kill old Hepplethwaite!" he roared, and slammed a coffin lid down in anger.

"They've shown me up to make money. Sold me for a mess of potash, like the chap in Clara's bible..... how can I face folk now? I'm done for... a figure of fun. I'll throw meself in t'cutting. It'll ruin me business, this." The poor chap flung himself into an old armchair and sobbed his heart out.

Joshua got to know the news when Bob Kearsley rang him at the linen mill.

"Who the hell would do a trick like that, Bob?" said Joshua. "Poor old Stanley's going to be disgraced. And what the hell Clara will do, I don't know. She 's so straightlaced, it'll kill her."

"It's not only Stanley and his missus, it's the club, too." went on Bob. "We're mentioned as well, and it's not complimentary. It's a pack of bloody lies, of course. But mud sticks. I reckon that Stanley's blabbed the story to someone when he was half-cut, and they've added to it to incriminate the club. Be prepared for a call from the league, Joshua."

An hour later a furious Stanley was in Joshua's office, accusing him of writing the article. Joshua handed him a glass.

"Here, get this down thee, lad, and give over cussing. I've read it, and up to a point it's all true. You made a bloody fool of yourself down in Wales, didn't you? But you know as well as I do that Dai Owen never turned out for Rovers, or came anywhere near the club. Do you think that I'd invent stuff like that against meself? Use your brains lad."

The scout was too upset to see the sense of Joshua's argument. He was a disgraced man. He had to blame someone. It made him feel better. Joshua was pacing the office, getting more angry every second. "When I discover who did this to us, I'll string him up by his meat and two veg from the cross bar at Rovers' ground." he raged. Then the phone rang. It was the secretary of the rugby league from the headquarters at Leeds. He told Joshua that Bramfield Rovers had brought the game into disrepute. There would be an official enquiry. Joshua hung up the receiver slowly. He had never given up a secret hope that at the last second the rugby league hierarchy would help them financially, even though they had told the club that it couldn't be done. That was the end of that dream. He reached for the bottle.

"I'll have a brandy as well. How is it that when you're down and out there's always some bugger to boot you in the backside with his clogs?"

Chapter Eight

Morgan the Voice

Stanley Keighley was sitting in front of the parlour fire making toast on a long toasting fork. The shock of the newspaper revelation had affected his usual hearty appetite, and he was smoking heavily, lighting one cigarette after another. It was late afternoon on the day after the news had broken, and toast and dripping was his first meal of the day. Clara was still at her mother's, she had left Stanley several times since their marriage, but this time he had a gut feeling that it would be quite a while before she returned, if she returned at all. He knew very well that he wasn't the perfect husband, but after all, he was only fond of a few drinks now and then. He was hardly the philanderer and reprobate that his mother-in-law made him out to be. She disliked him and the feeling was mutual. He had once told her that he would do her one favour, even though he couldn't stand her, and that would be to bury her free of charge. Like Queen Victoria, she was not amused.

He was on his third slice of toast and dripping when the phone rang. Stanley was very suspicious, and stared at the new fangled machine for several seconds before he picked up the receiver. He had already had two calls from journalists that day wanting to expand on the story. He cautiously said "Who is it?"

"It's me, Stanley boyo, Morgan the voice."

It was a sing song welsh voice which Stanley immediately recognised.

"Dai Morgan? How are you lad?"

"I'm very well, Stanley, I've heard about your trouble, and I'm very sorry. I'm a sports journalist now, on the Daily Messenger. We were offered the story for our Sunday edition, but turned it down."

"Have you any idea who wrote it, Dai?"

"No boyo, but I intend to find out. Brace yourself for the weekend, I'm told it will be in at least three Sunday papers. I thought I'd better warn you."

"It'll put me in an early grave, and it will ruin me marriage. I'm done for, Dai lad. I might as well jump in canal. What with the team on the way out of the league, life's not worth living these days."

"Grit your teeth, Stanley bach, it will pass. If you found a new star for the team, wouldn't that help?"

"What the hell would we pay him with? Dripping butties and tapwashers? The club's as poor as the lice on Job's turkey, and they don't come any poorer than that, Dai."

"Well, I've found one for you. He's a stand-off half. Plays union for Harlequins, fast as a whippet he is, and tackles like a bulldog."

"What the hell does he want to come to Bramfield for, surely he knows the state we're in? The club's run out of brass."

"He's not interested in money. He's a man of independent means. He just fancies the league code. He's quite prepared to play trials. I've told him all about my time with the Rovers and he likes the idea."

"Not interested in brass? He must be barmy. I don't believe it."

"It's the truth, boyo. Anyway, if you give him a trial, you can't lose, and think of the attraction it will create and the extra gate money it will bring in. Think of it, it will capture the imagination of the town, an ex-public school chap with a double barrelled name, Walker-Smythe."

"Oh no, oh no! We've had enough flaming musical comedy. I'm not being the scapegoat again. Folks here won't take to a chap like that, anyway, neither will the players....."

"He's a grand chap, very ordinary, not stand offish at all...."

"I thought you said he were a stand-off? Make thee mind up!"

"An unintentional pun, boyo. Take a chance, Stanley, you've got nothing to lose. Besides, if Rovers don't take him, he'll go to Wigan or Leeds. With me being his friend, he promised he would give the Rovers first refusal. He'll be a winner, Stanley. Another Les Fairclough,[8] I'd say."

"You're joking!"

"No boyo, I'm deadly serious."

"Just a trial then? No expenses?"

"Nothing, it won't cost the club anything. I owe the Rovers a favour. They were good to me and I want to see those old days return. Remember when we won at Wembley? We were proud of Rovers that day, weren't we? I'll never forget you dancing in your pyjamas in the hotel corridor nursing a bottle of rum!"

"Don't you start, Dai Morgan. Don't go mentioning that to anyone, or I'll be in flipping papers again. Ee, I'll never forget that tackle you made on their loose forrard as he was going under the posts....Aye, appen a trial would do no harm, but I'll have to consult the directors first. Another Leslie Fairclough, did you say? Well, you should know a player when you see one, Dai. When can he turn out?"

"No time like the present, what about this Saturday, are you at home?"

"Yes, Wigan. Baptism of fire eh?"

"Well, why not? If he plays well against them he'll do. What do you say, then Stanley?"

"I think it's worth a do. I'll get in touch with 'owd Joshua. Ring me back tonight and I'll give you the verdict."

"'Till tonight, Stanley. Tell Mr Hepplethwaite and the Kearsley brothers that Dai Morgan has found them a rugby league star of the future."

The humiliated scout was caught between two emotions. His first reaction was to regret that he had agreed to pass the news on to the club. He should have told Dai Morgan to approach the directors himself. If it all went wrong, 'muggins' would be blamed. Another blunder. This natural reaction was soon diluted by a flush of acute optimism. Perhaps it would be a chance to salvage some pride? If the player did turn out to be a star, at least he could always claim that he had a hand in discovering him, even if he had only acted as a 'middle man'. And surely Dai wouldn't recommend anyone unless he was sure they were professional material? Morgan had been a great attraction at Bramfield, one of the best union converts Stanley had poached from the welsh valleys. Not only that, he had been a great favourite of his mother's, for she loved a good tenor, and Dai had a fine voice, in great demand for concerts all over Lancashire. He would never forget him singing 'Ave Maria' at her eightieth birthday party.... It brought a lump to his throat. That sort of man would never play a dirty trick, surely?

Joshua was enjoying a hot cup of cocoa, sitting by his office fire. It was a bitter cold day, and his waterworks problem was playing him up again. That morning he had visited a specialist for a second opinion. The verdict that it was caused by severe stress and worry did nothing to comfort him. The specialist advised him to face the inevitable: he must accept that the Rovers were doomed. The theory being that acceptance would lead to a gradual lessening of the symptoms, and eventual recovery. He was further advised to close the club down as soon as possible, and then take a long period of rest. The medical opinion was that if he kept on feeding his anxious state, the condition would worsen, and he would need an operation. Furthermore, the specialist told him that he was on the edge of a nervous breakdown. It was 'Hobson's Choice'. His melancholia was disturbed by the strident tone of the telephone which agitated his sensitized nerves. His hand shook as he lifted the receiver. Upon hearing Stanley's familiar voice, he immediately thought the worst.

"What the hell's gone wrong this time, lad?" It was the remark of a depressed man. Stanley assured him that all was well, and repeated what he had been told by Dai Morgan. It was a shot in the arm to Joshua. From being in the depths of despair, he was suddenly back to his vibrant form as the chairman of Bramfield Rovers.

"Why not Stanley lad, why not?" he enthused when the scout had finished talking. "I've been told to wind the Rovers up as a going concern. Doctor's orders. Well, you've given me a straw to cling to, lad, we'll go down fighting, six shooters blazing. We've got nowt to lose. I'm speaking on behalf of my fellow directors when I tell you to get back to Morgan. I want this lad up here pronto, do you hear? We don't want him changing his mind and going to some other club. And whatever you do, don't mention his name to anyone. I'm relying on you, Stanley lad, to keep 'mum'. Keep thee gob buttoned. Think on. We'll call him A.N. Other on the programme. I'll get in touch with the local paper to tell them we've got a prominent rugby union trialist turning out, and I want you to get your skates on lad, and get round to Albert Heneberry and tell him to put the word out to the supporters' club. We want the news spreading. Wigan always bring a good crowd with them, and I want an extra special turn out of our own speccies..... by gum lad, you don't know what joy you've given me. Where there's

life, there's hope, and who knows, he might be another Les Fairclough....
appen he might, stranger things have happened at sea. Get to it Stanley,
owd cock, and ring me tonight at our house."

He replaced the receiver and took another warming gulp of cocoa.
Wind up the Rovers, indeed? Next week, perhaps....but they'd have one
last fling before that fateful day. They bloody would an all!
The news travelled from office to pit face, from mill floor to dole queue
and from tap room to street corner. The debut of a new player was
always an important talking point, a ray of light in the depressing gloom
of an industrial town. Soon, the town was buzzing with excitement.
Stanley had passed on the directors' agreement to Dai Morgan and the
welshman had promised to wire the chairman at his office. The
telegram duly arrived at Joshua's office on the Wednesday morning.

WALKER-SMYTHE. ARRIVE 10.30 A.M.
BRAMFIELD CENTRAL. THURSDAY.
DAI MORGAN.
The three directors were chatting excitedly as the train pulled into the
station on the Thursday morning.

"It's like waiting for Father Christmas to come." said Bob Kearsley.

"I can't help feeling excited meself." said Joshua as the passengers
left the train. "There's nothing like a new player to get the adrenalin
going." The directors stared eagerly at the face of every young man.
The trialist was not on the train.

When Joshua arrived back at the office, he met the uniformed
telegram boy riding into the mill yard on his bicycle.

"Telegram for you, Mr Hepplethwaite. Will I wait while you answer
it?" Joshua eagerly tore it open. It read:

WALKER-SMYTHE. ARRIVE 10.30 A.M.
FRIDAY INSTEAD. DAI MORGAN.

Joshua took the lad into his office and wrote out a reply which read:

IMPERATIVE FRIDAY A.M.
NO LATER.
PRACTICE ROVERS' GROUND.

P.M. DO NOT FAIL.
HEPPLETHWAITE.

Joshua gave the lad a tip and told him to pedal like hell back to the telegraph office.

On the Friday morning the three directors repeated their vigil at the station. The train pulled into the platform and once again they eagerly watched the passengers making their way to the exit barrier. Once again, the trialist failed to appear. Joshua stormed into the station telegraph office, and sent the following wire:

WHAT THE HELL IS GOING ON? HEPPLETHWAITE.

This was cruel. Joshua knew in his heart that he couldn't stand much more of it. He paced up and down his office unable to concentrate on anything else except the disappointment. If the 'missus' knew about this, she'd play hell with me, he thought to himself as he stared out of the office window into the winter gloom.

"Mr Hepplethwaite, a telegram for you. I've told the lad to wait." It was Martha, his secretary. Joshua took it from her eagerly and tore it open. It read:

ARRANGEMENTS CHANGED. PLAYER ARRIVES BY CAR TONIGHT. KEIGHLEY'S HOUSE. DAI MORGAN.

The lad asked Joshua if he wanted to reply. "Nay lad. What I've got to say wouldn't be accepted by your office. I'd be done for using foul language. I'm like a ruddy puppet, dangled on a string by the hand of fate."

The telegram lad gave him a funny look. Joshua poured himself a brandy. He was in a foul mood.

Chapter Nine

Learning The Ropes

The drama now switches to Arkwright Sidings, home of the Keighley family. Clara was back with her husband, 'but only as long as he behaved himself and didn't show her up anymore'. That was her condition, but she knew in her heart that Stanley couldn't stay away from the booze for long. The truth was, she had taken all she could from her mother, who was like a gramophone record when the needle sticks, playing the same old tune over and over again, ad nauseam. At least Stanley didn't give her earache. Heartache, maybe, but then appen all men were the same. She was cogitating along these lines as she cleaned the parlour. The place was in a mess, meat dripping all over the kitchen range, toast bits in the hearth rug and dirty feet marks on the linoleum. But wasn't that men the world over? "You can't leave them five minutes without the place getting into a mess . . . . . What a state, look at it . . . . ecky thump, he's even knocked over the aspidistra in the old art pot great aunt Polly Ann gave us on us wedding day . . . . dear dear . . . . and he's not even cleaned up the soil, would you believe? And look at this cigarette ash! What would that man do without me?"

Stanley could hear his wife's mutterings as he washed the dishes at the slop stone under sufferance. What would he do without her? That was a laugh! He'd go off gallivanting to Blackpool for a start, dancing at the tower. Appen a bit o' wenching. Bit o' dancing on North Pier, then there were the oyster bars, and the golden mile and appen a visit to his mate, Alf Ellaby, who owned the Veevers Arms. He was getting carried away into daydreams, playing the game of 'what might have been' when he was brought back to stark reality by the caustic edge of Clara's tongue.

"Watch them bone handle knives in the hot water, Stanley! They belonged to me mother's cousin. Ermentrude, who married a vicar. They were her pride and joy, them knives."

She was scrubbing away assiduously when a large Buick pulled up outside. She opened the door to Bob Kearsley, who was soon followed by his brother Bert who had arrived in a beautifully polished Rover. What a field day for the busy bodies and window peepers across the street. The light was still good enough for them to see the procession of prestige vehicles, which was soon supplemented by the arrival of Joshua in a Rolls Royce. It was as good as a wedding to inquisitive eyes which could not fail to see the severe look upon the chairman's face, and the purposefulness of his walk to the Keighley's front door. This was serious business. Stanley Keighley was going to get the sack from the club, that was it. It was obvious, said the woman at number twelve to the woman at number ten as they stood side by side, unashamedly staring at the Keighley residence. But what they thought when an open tourer turned up, driven by a young man in a red and blue striped blazer was anyone's guess - and the woman with him.... well.....!

"No decent woman would dress like that, she's showing all she's got", said the woman at number twelve in a disgusted tone of voice.

"And she's got a lot, she's a hussy, is that one." said the woman at number ten. "A scarlet woman!"

Clara let the young couple into the house. The young man introduced himself "I'm Percy Walker-Smythe, and this is my fiance, Cynthia Trotter. Am I at the home of Mr Stanley Keighley?"

"Come in lad, and you lass." said Clara without fuss.

"So you've arrived, have you?" it was Joshua in his best no- nonsense mood. "We thought you were coming early doors on Thursday."

"My apologies, Mr...?"

"Hepplethwaite, lad. I'm chairman of the Rovers' rugby league club, and these are my co-directors, Mr Bob and Mr Bert Kearsley. So what kept thee? We're all business men, we haven't time to be hanging about on railway stations on wild goose chases."

"I do apologise, Mr Applewhite. I had to tidy up my business affairs, you know. The delay was unavoidable, I'm afraid."

"The name's Hepplethwaite. Dai Morgan says you're a stand-off. Coming so late has given us no time to give you a few lessons in the rudiments of the game. We could have gone to the ground and had a practice with a couple of the players."

"The lad's here now, Joshua, and we'll have to make the most of it." said Bob.

"Do you know anything about rugby league?" asked Bert.

"I've seen a couple of games at Leeds, I was up doing a spot of shooting on the moors. A jolly exciting game, I thought. I'm very keen to do well in professional rugger, aren't I darling?"
Cynthia beamed at him. "Oh, I know you'll be a success Percy. He's talked about nothing else on the way up. He's very good, you know.... aren't you petal?"

"You're embarrassing me, old girl," said Percy, squeezing her hand. Stanley Keighley gave an bewildered cough. Clara said she would mash the tea. Joshua stared at his boots.

"It's a lot different to union, Mr Walker-Smythe." said Bert Kearsley.

"I say, why don't you drop the Walker and just call me Smythe? Or if you like, Percy will do."
Joshua was looking the trialist up and down with a critical eye.

"There's not much of you lad. In fact, there's more meat on our Fred's whippet. Dai Morgan tells us you're a flyer."

"That's right, Mr Applewhite, I'm very fast."

"And yon fancy woman looks a fast piece, an all." said Clara to her self as she mashed the tea.

"Now let's get down to brass tacks, Mr Smith. Sit thee down, pair of you." ordered the chairman.

"Smythe, Mr Applewhite, rhymes with dive and Clive, don't you know?"

"Now let's put cards on table, so you'll know where you stand if we do sign you. I think you know the score already, Mr Smith."

"I am aware of the unfortunate predicament which Bramfield Rovers are in. By the way, I dislike being pedantic, but it *is* Smythe."
Joshua, who was on a very short fuse indeed, exploded. "Smith or Smythe - shit or shite, what the bloody hell does it matter? I've come here to talk rugby league, not to have a lecture on elocution. We're plain folk in Bramfield, and we speak us minds. Now let's get down to it, okay? I'll not beat about bush, we're living from day to day at the club. The chances of survival aren't much better than nil.

73

Anyhow, it's my duty as club chairman to make sure that you know the rates of pay. Mr Kearsley, you're more conversant with it than me."

Bob Kearsley, well known in the game for his encyclopaedic memory on all matters appertaining to rugby league, as well as being a monologuist at local 'do's' in the Stanley Holloway style, was only too pleased to reel off the rates.

"The table of suggested rates for 1935/1936 season is as follows: This applies to the first team only as the 'A' team had to be disbanded. Home win, 3 pounds 5 shillings. Home lose, 1 pound 10 shillings. Away win versus Lancashire clubs, 3 pounds 15 shillings. Away lose versus Lancashire clubs, 1 pound 15 shillings. Away win Yorkshire or at Barrow, 4 pounds 5 shillings. Away lose Yorkshire or at Barrow, 2 pounds. Reserves will be paid losing money. If a player is selected for an international match, he will receive 8 pounds in a lump sum. If selected for a county match, he will receive three pounds in a lump sum.

Now to compensation for injury caused on the field of play. If married or having dependants, 2 pounds 5 shillings. If single, 1 pound 17 shillings and 6 pence. Now then, we come to tea money: This will be allowed at the rate of 2 shillings and 6 pence for all clubs on away matches, other than Liverpool Stanley, Widnes, Salford, Broughton, Oldham, Warrington and Leigh. If meals are provided by the club, no money will be paid. I should have also mentioned, that in the case of drawn games, a home draw is paid as a lose and a away draw as a win. Should a player obtain international status, individual terms will be negotiated with the committee."

"Thanks, Mr Kearsley", said Joshua, being extremely formal in the circumstances. "Now lets hear about you lad. Mrs Keighley's mashed the tea, good hearted lass that she is. Have you been playing long?"

"Ever since I was a young chap, Mr Applewhite. I was in the first team at Harrow and went on to Old Archeonians, a local rugger side, then to Harlequins."

"Well, I can't say as I've heard of you lad, but we don't keep up with 'union news in these parts. They play it up here, of course, but they tend to copy the league style, give the ball plenty of air. After all, it's called the handling code. It's kicking what kills 'union, they're too scared to pass in case they get tackled and lose the ball. It's not a spectator sport like our game."

"You're quite right there Joshua", agreed Bert Kearsley, "I'd sooner watch Jim Sullivan play tiddley winks than watch 'union. The balls more out of play than in."

"I heartily agree, gentlemen" said the triallist. "I look upon myself as a pioneer, and I believe that rugby league will conquer new boundaries, and I hope to be a part of that progress."

"Well, before thee conquer new boundaries, let's see you conquer Wigan first. Let's show you how to play the ball." commented Joshua.

"That is the procedure after one is tackled, I presume?"

"Aye, as I've just said, when a player's tackled in 'union, there's a chance he can lose the ball when they all pile on, boots slashing like scythes in corn,they're more like marauding tribesmen in the jungle than rugby players. Upper class hooligans, I call 'em. In our game, when a man's grounded, the game stops and he plays the ball back to the acting half-back, as we call him. This is difficult for 'union players to learn, so I'm going to give you a few lessons when we've had us tea.... if Clara won't object?"

"Feel free, Mr Hepplethwaite." said Mrs Keighley.

"I wonder what we can use for the ball." said Joshua. Stanley's eyes had lit on Cynthia's buxom chest. By gum, she's a big lass, he was thinking to himself. But Clara spotted him with her beady eyes.

"What are you gawping at, Stanley? Are you paying attention? The chairman was just wondering what to use for a ball."

"Aye......... so were I, lass! Should I go and get me hard 'at?"

"We'll think of summat." said the Chairman, taking a cup of tea from Clara. "I should have called at ground for a ball."

"Will you take a cup o' tea, miss? What do you do for a living?" asked Clara.

"I'm a designer of clothes", said Cynthia, using this as a cue to stand up and twirl round like a model, revealing her thighs. "I plan to open a boutique in Bramfield."

"A what luv, a boot shop?"

"No, no, Mrs Keighley, a dress shop, sartorial elegance for the ladies of the town."

"Oh, you mean pinnies and aprons?"

"Not quite, Mrs K, high class fashions. Mr K will be able to buy you the latest parisian gown."

75

"Nay, miss, there's not that sort of brass in these parts, but I would like a nice dress, meself. It's the fifteenth anniversary of the women's guild soon, and I fancy a new outfit. Have you got a tape measure on you miss?"

"Use Stanley's", said Joshua with heavy sarcasm.

"Oh, is Mr K a gentlemen's outfitter then?" asked Cynthia.

"No lass, he's an undertaker. Let's postpone this dressmaking talk and get on with teaching the lad how to play the bloody ball."

"Language, please, in my house!"

"Sorry Clara lass, and you miss. I'm on edge, you see."

"Oh, don't apologise, I can swear with the best of them, can't I, sweety pie?" Cynthia gave a high pitched giggle which made her bust wobble provocatively and Stanleys eyes almost leave their sockets.

"Not half, petal! Especially when some clumsy clot knocks your gin and tonic over in the club house. You'd make a bargee blush."

"Really! Well I never! Such talk in our parlour!"

Clara gave a disgusted shake of the head as she poured the tea.

"Can you play in other positions, young man?" Asked Bob Kearsley.

"Yes, Mr Kearsley, I've played centre and full back on occasions."

"Well, that shows versatility" said brother Bert.

Joshua was showing signs of irritability. "Now sup thee tea up and we'll get down to basic principles. Stanley lad, get your prize marrow from back yard."

"What, and ruin its chances for allotment show next week? It's in for Mayor's prize. Not ruddy likely. I'ts like a son to me."

"Are you a Rovers' man or a bloody horticulturist? Did Napoleon in his hour of crisis worry about winning a prize for biggest marrow?"

"I don't think he had one, Mr Hepplethwaite." said Stanley.

"Come on, we haven't got all neet, we haven't got a ball, so bring it pronto!" While Stanley was down the back yard with his beloved marrow, Clara couldn't resist bringing up the matter of the new dress. She didn't approve of Miss Trotter, but her desire for a new dress overcome her disapproval. "Appen you've got a few samples of material, Miss Trotter? When men have done with rugby, perhaps we can arrange for you to come round sometime. I've been saving up, you see, and I'd feel real proud to have one made by a London designer."

"Certainly, Mrs Keighley, it'd be a pleasure".

76

"Are you familiar with the north miss." asked Bob Kearsley politely, trying to make conversation.

"We studied the north of England at school. We learned all about the Industrial Revolution, and I can remember particularly some of the wonderful inventions that came from Yorkshire." Joshua pricked up his ears at the mention of the rival county.

Yorkshire was like the proverbial red rag to a bull to him. "They weren't bad lass, but Lancashire is the best county in the north. We've got the best inventors, and we're the best at cricket, too.... and best brass bands.... finest ale brewers, best hosses, and you can't get a better black pudding anywhere, and talking of inventions, what about the Spinning Jenny for the mills? Nay, we're streets ahead of them, Miss."

"But be fair, Joshua lad." said Bert,"It were a Yorkshire man what invented the lavatory seat, tha knows."

"Aye, appen it were, but it were a Lancashire man what put the hole in it."

Joshua tapped his head, "It's brains, miss.... I'll have to go down yard lass, I've been taken short again."

Clara gave him one of her cold withering looks. For once Joshua was unrepentant.

"I'm sorry lass, but I reckon southerners pass water same as northerners.... And I'll fetch that husband of yours, while I'm at it. I don't think he can bear to part with that marrow."

As soon as the chairman had left the parlour, Clara said "You'll have to excuse Mr Hepplethwaite, Miss. He's a big hearted man, but he forgets where he is sometimes."

"Oh, I find him a real darling, Mrs K" said Cynthia.

"You'll find him a grand boss, lad." said Bob to the new stand-off. "He's' what we call a 'rum 'un' up here lad, is Joshua. But he's got a heart of gold. The players think the world of him. Ee, by gum, I'll never forget him giving us a song at that big do we had after Wembley. He'd give his last drop of blood for Rovers."

Joshua returned, followed by Stanley, carrying his prize vegetable. The scout had a face like a scolded child.

"Stop sulking, Stanley." said Joshua. "Grit thee teeth and think of Rovers. It might still win, anyway. It weighs a bloody ton."

"No chance now it's been taken away from mother plant. Another week and it would have done. I reckon we'll have to eat it instead."

Clara thought that was a wonderful idea.

"That's right, Stanley, we'll stuff it with some mince and onions, it's a good dish is that, with a bit....."

Clara's culinary dialogue was interrupted by Joshua's impatient cough. The chairman called for order and said "I'll now show Mr Walker how to play the ball. Stanley, pick up the marrow and fall on the floor. We'll pretend you've been tackled. Now I stand behind him as the acting half back. Are you with me young man?"

The parlour was almost bursting at the seams, and the floorboards groaned as Stanley's vast bulk hit the linoleum.

"Now watch carefully what Stanley does with his foot. He's heeled it back to me, and my job is to pass it to a team mate known as the first receiver..... get it? Come on Bob lad, you can be the first receiver." Bob, who was handing round his pickle jar, took his place alongside Joshua, who looked at him with disapproval. "Put the jar down, Bob lad. No self respecting player eats pickles, this is a serious practice, even though we are in a parlour."

The procedure was repeated three times, with much grunting and groaning. If Joshua and company had been seen by directors of other clubs, it would have been the joke of the century,but Percy Walker-Smythe studied the pantomime with the earnestness of a man witnessing an event of paramount importance to the world. And now it was his turn. He was handed the marrow, and after a few trials and errors,he mastered the heeling of the ball to the acting half back. Joshua was relishing his role as coach. He announced, "Now we'll reverse it. Bob will play the ball,and I'll be the acting half back, and you lad will be the first reciever". Clara and Stanley moved the furniture around to accommodate the trio more comfortably. The pass from Joshua was dropped by Percy, as was the second, only this time the marrow split open onto the linoleum. Stanley was furious. "I'm making no apologies for swearing, Clara lass, you come here Mr Hepplethwaite and ruin me chances of winning a prize with me marrer and now you've buggered it up and we can't even stuff it."

The Chairman took no notice. "Aw reet Clara, bring us in a turnip." The scenario was repeated until the trialist felt happy with this new aspect of rugby. "I think you've got it now, Percy lad," said the chairman. Has any one got any ideas how to make it more realistic?

Cynthia, who was finding her role as spectator very boring, was keen to join in. "I'd love to have a go Mr H. I played in a girls rugger team and the boys were keen to play us."

"I bet they were 'an all lass" said Joshua with a grin "I wouldn't mind scrumming down with thee meself."

"Jolly good show Mr H!, I'll tackle you then I'll oppose you and play the ball. What ho! I say isn't rugby league super fun!

In the resulting melee, Bob Kearsley got severe cramp and had to be carried to his car by his co-directors, but not before Joshua had given the new lad strict instructions to be at the ground 'early doors' the next day.

Cynthia was put up on the Keighley's couch and Percy was given a bed in the spare room, completely unaware that the last occupant had been a corpse laid to rest that very day. As Clara made her supper cocoa, she wondered what on earth the vicar would have made of it all.

Chapter Ten

Going To The Match

Albert Heneberry, the council comedian, and chairman of the supporters' club, was standing under the shadow of 'Uncle' Cohen's three brass balls in Union Street. The pawnbroker was the busiest tradesman in Bramfield, as in all northern towns. There were no less than six similar shops in the area. Albert was a flamboyant character with a red face, a beer belly held up by short legs. He wore a grubby 'mac' and a green, flat cap. It was a cold but dry day. Ideal for the match. This was the usual meeting place for Albert and his pals. They turned up one by one. When all had mustered they ventured into the 'spit and sawdust' of the canal vaults, a most uncomfortable pub but noted for its friendliness and as a great 'making out' place for rugby fans. Albert was in the chair. He always was on a Saturday. His mates were unlikely companions for one of his social standing. His chemist's sundries business had almost put him on a level with the big business men and industrialists of the district. But they were not his kind of people. It was rumoured that his great uncle Nat Heneberry, who had invented the Do-It Yourself Enema Engine, had left Albert all his money. He could retire any time he chose to. Not so his mates, Big Billy Hagan, Ambrose Dolan, and Bert Pilkington. Billy and Ambrose were night soil men. Their's was the lowest and most unsavoury occupation one could imagine. They cleaned out the human effluent from the backyard privies, and, as the name implies, the job was usually performed at night. Although flush lavatories had been introduced into the town, very many streets were still without them.

Albert insisted on 'treating' them all, and often ended up being touched for gills of mild beer by men who knew of his generosity. He loved an audience and he didn't mind paying out a few bob for it. Besides, he genuinely wanted to buy them drinks, for he was starkly aware of the meagre existences of most of them. Albert set the ball rolling with a joke "Owd Fred Postlethwaite had a bad corn on his foot. He went to one of them chirrypodolists and he tells Fred that his feet are mucky.

"Are they muckier than thyne?" asked our Fred.

"Of course they are!" said the chirrypodolist.

"Aagh, well, I'm older than thee." said Fred. The joke caused great amusement until someone said "I don't know what we're laughing at, we'll get etten alive by Wigan."

"I bet you Ellaby runs in six agin us" said Bert.

"He's not as good since he left St. Helens" said Ambrose.

"Appen so but he's still a danger" opined Albert.

"He'd be dangerous sittin int' bath would Alf." agreed Bert.

"Hope springs eternal" remarked big Billy.

"The run of defeats has to end sometime." said Bert.

"I wish I were as optimistic as you Billy" said Albert.

"42-2 agin Barrow – another good hiding, unless Wigin play their third team we're doomed."

"Still, we'll never desert the lads will we? once a die-hard always a die-hard." Alberts words summed up the feelings of all concerned.

He consulted his gold watch, which hung on a chain from his waist coat pocket. "Lets get going, lads. It's a fine day for a walk up to the ground."

There was a short cut through the market hall. It was no place for a hungry man, for it was full of gastronomic delights. Black pudding and muffin stalls, hot pea saloons, hot drink stalls catering for people on low incomes, and all manner of edible goods. The smell of offal and sawdust mingled with Elliman's rub and camphor balls, while the butcner's and fish merchants were sweeping the waste products away from their stalls then swilling the stone flags with hot soapy water. Liquorice root and cinder toffee were two of the delicacies to be found in Bramfield market, while bottles of Liquorice Allsorts, Pontefract Cakes, and Owd Ned's Winter Mixture, fraternised on the shelves with

81

Sherbet and Colt's Foot Rock. Due to the slump, only half the stalls were occupied. The market would fill up later, when the women folk would come to the weekly Saturday auctions at the butcher's stalls, who sold off the meat cheaply to prevent it going off. "Hang on lads", said Albert "I'll just get a penny bag of tripe bits".

He liberally sprinkled the delicacy with salt and pepper. "It's better than caviar, is this, and I've had that in Midland Hotel in Manchester."

As they reached the dirt patch outside the market, they heard the cries of men playing their favourite games: pitch and toss, long distance spitting, and 'how long can you keep a ferret down your trousers?' Old shawled grandmothers would tell their grandchildren that it was a den of iniquity, a place where dubious characters wasted their time. A tea stall, with a huge urn that looked as if it could have catered for a whole regiment, was belching out steam and dispensing tea to wan faced women. For many, it was a Saturday treat. A Plymouth Brethren preacher was telling them to repent and alongside him was a black man playing a ukulele and singing "How're you're going keep 'em down on the farm now that they've seen Paree?" Owd Nell, a lodging house women, played her one string fiddle and sang to its accompaniment. She went in for the classics and always attracted an appreciative audience who loved to hear her play hymns and arias.

Outside the Collier's Arms public house was gathered a large party of Wigan spectators clad in cherry and white mufflers, all eating hot pies and pasties with mushy peas.

"It's not a match for them", said Ambrose, "It's more like a day out at Blackpool".

The local Echo and Express were popular papers in the town, and 'Soft Billy', as he was known, was the paper seller. He was a 'Desperate Dan' sort of character, who had been brought up in common lodging houses, but he was no fool, and he always had an answer. He handed one of his regulars a paper. It was the mid-day edition, but the man waved it aside:

"I'm not taking any more papers, Billy. I've bought a radio instead."
Billy bawled at him:
"You can wipe your backside on an Echo, but you can't on a radio!"
The clanking and hooting of a tram car as it nosed its way through the crowded street mingled with the shouts and laughter of the rival

supporters who swarmed over the cobbles oblivious to the approach of the slow moving vehicle. Many a man had received a nasty bang from a tram as he staggered from a pub after a Saturday dinner time session. A familiar figure to the Bramfield supporters was waiting at a stop. In fact it was true to say that she was well known to legions of fans from all over the north, a legend. Old Ma Cornish was a notorious character at Marl Heights ground, as was her umbrella. As the tram trundled noisily to the stop she raised the brolly aloft and shouted as a crowd rushed to board the vehicle.

"Have you no manners you lot! Haven't you heard of ladies first?" Her fierce words acted like a magic wand. The mob parted like the Red Sea before the Israelites and Ma stepped aboard daintily. A Jekyll and Hyde character, during the week she was an inoffensive woman surrounded by cats, on match days metamorphosis took place, transforming her into a dragon and a very biased one at that. Her regular position on the ground was by the players tunnel and many an opponent had received a belt on the head from Ma's brolly. On one occasion she had gone too far and hit the referee. The club were warned by the league authorities and the Rovers committee had banned her from the ground for a month. Ma Cornish was completely unrepentant and her brolly was likely to flash like a sword from its scabbard whenever the opportunity of retribution upon a Rovers opponent presented itself.

Good humoured banter and ribald remarks were the order of the day as both sets of spectators headed towards the steep street which led up to the high open ground on which the Rovers' field was situated. This street was noted for its traders, who set stalls out on the cobbled setts - haberdashery men with trays of buttons and collar studs, Dandelion and Burdock stalls, and possibly the most popular on match days, the chap who sold Uncle Joe's Mint Balls, which were guaranteed to warm you up. This was a street of mean boarding houses which were always full, and several of the residents were sitting on the steps watching the crowd go by. A Salvation Army band was proceeding towards them, and this caused a diversity of reaction. The older folk in the crowd joined in the hymn while the younger, more cheeky section made irreverent remarks. Albert couldn't resist a joke, even though he was a sponsor of the band.

"Do you save fallen women?" he asked the girl with the tambourine.

'THAT'LL LEARN YOU TO SEND ONE OF OUR LADS OFF!'

Well, save one for me, will you?"

None of his pals laughed, it was the oldest joke in the book, but it caused great merriment amongst the Wigan contingent. "They'll laugh at owt in Wigan", said Big Billy, who was eating a chip butty. "They even think George Formby's funny."

The mention of the famous Wiganer's name set the crowd singing:

'I'm leaning on a lampost at the corner of the street....'

One of the Wigan Speccies played a jaws harp and another a comb and paper. Albert pulled out a mouth organ from his waist coat pocket and joined in. They were rival spectators united by music before the match, but it would be a different story once the action started. There would be no love lost then.

The street was so steep that many of the crowd were puffing and blowing by the time they had got halfway up, and a strategically situated pub with the homely name of the 'Comfortable Gill' was a haven of rest. It was also a good place for 'Singing Sam', one of the lodging house men who always busked on match days. He was a typical Yates' Wine Lodge tenor, and specialised in victorian ballads. His favourite was 'Queen of The Earth', which demanded a good voice. The high notes were too much for Sam, and he would break off in the middle of the song to bawl at the kids who were usually playing around his feet. It was Albert's custom to bring Sam a gill of mild, and again he couldn't resist cracking one of his hairy old gags. "Can thee sing the 'Refrain From Spitting', Sam?" The old tramp always laughed at Albert's jokes, because he knew when he was on to a good thing. The man with the placard which stated '**The end is nigh!**', was a source of great amusement to the Wigan supporters, but was not appreciated by the Rovers' 'speccies.

As Albert and his cronies mounted the summit of the hill, a flurry of snow hit them. The weather had suddenly turned cold. "By gum, it's colder than Blackstone Edge", said Albert, rubbing his hands vigorously. "It could make the going very slushy, this stuff that's falling." The charabanc park was pitted with potholes.

"It's a run down looking place is this", said one of the Wigan fans. A lot of their mates had arrived in charabancs and a sea of cherry and white mufflers made its way to the turnstiles. The longest queue was at a turnstile which sported a board bearing the legend 'Unemployed

Half-Price' . Some of the men had whippets on strings, and many a dogfight had broken out on the popular side terrace.

Albert said "Well, I think we've got a better crowd than usual, lads. Owd Joshua and his directors will be pleased. I hope this new lad shows his paces. We'll need a few attractions to keep the speccies coming, there's nowt like new players to wet the 'speccies' appetite."

Ambrose said "I bet he's more like a ballet dancer than a rugby player. I think he's one of them nancy boys from a public school."

"I heard he's played at 'Twickers', said Big Billy, showing off his knowledge of elite sporting arenas. Ambrose blew loudly into his muffler and said:

"Knickers to Twickers! Them's not rugby grounds what they have down there. They soften 'em before they play then they won't hurt themselves. Watersheddings, Post Office Road, Lawkholme Lane, them's proper grounds."

"I suppose we have to give the southerners some credit for inventing the game of rugby." said Bert grudgingly.

"Nay" said Albert "it were a Yorkshire lad that invented it."

"You're wrong there Albert," said Bert "it was at rugby school, I've read about it in public library."

"That's as maybe, I'll tell you the story if you want." Albert took a nip from his pocket flask. "It was like this, see. Rugby Public School was overrun by rats. It was all that posh grub that caused it. Oysters, horses doovers, port wine and caviar. Rats love it. It's a well-known fact that southerners don't make good rat catchers so the headmaster had to send for Seth Bladderwart from Featherstone. The great plague in London was caused by rats. They didn't have one in Wigan and Halifax did they? Even Widnes escaped. Which shows you that rat catching has always been a northern skill – – –."

"What's all this got to do with the game of rugby, Albert?" asked a mystified Bert.

"The only rats I know in the game are the referees."

Albert blew loudly on his hanky and took a pinch of snuff.

"– – – If you give me time I'll tell you owd cock. You see when Seth went down to visit the headmaster he put a proposition to him. Seth had always wanted to be a gentleman – – – he had aspirations above his station you might say, – – so he thinks if it's too late for him he'd turn his son Fred into a gentleman instead, so he says he'll exterminate the rodents if Fred can be a pupil. Well the head had no choice, the rats were taking over, so he agrees. Seth fettled the rats in an afternoon and so Fred Bladderwart enrolled as a scholar at Rugby. He was a big lad having been brought up on the best chuck, like chip butties, dripping and cow heels, so he soon becomes the star of the football team; one day he picks up the ball and belts off to put it down between the goal posts. Of course he'd been doing this for years, back home in Yorkshire on the coal tips. So it's true to say that the game was invented on the slag heaps of Featherstone and not the playing fields of Rugby School."

"It's a rum story is that" said Bert, scratching his head.

"Aye and you're bloody rummer still if you believe it." said Ambrose with a guffaw.

"Albert's the editor of "Billy's Weekly Liar" didn't you know?"

His pals grunted in approval, and made their way through the turnstiles which were being manned by unpaid labour. When they were in the ground they were greeted by Joshua Hepplethwaite. "Hello lads. We've a fair gate today. I'm right proud of these lads at the turnstiles, they're working for nowt. Thanks for organising it for me, Albert. You've been a great help, lad. I always said we had the best Supporters' Club in league. If we survive, me and my directors will make it up to your lads. Appen we'll put on a hot do for them at Christmas, if we've still got a club."

"Don't worry about that, Joshua, the supporters' club will back you to the last. If the Rovers go down, we'll go down with 'em."

He shook Joshua's hand warmly. It was comradeship in the face of adversity. Joshua put his arm around Albert's shoulders and whispered, quite audibly "Up Rovers! and giving a V sign shouted for all to hear "and up thee Jeremiah Crumpsall – traitor!".

Chapter 11

The Match

'Woodbine Willie' Birch had been trainer at Marl Heights for sixteen seasons. A small, scraggy man with a face like a weasel, and a voice like a fog horn, Willie was the keeper of the magic sponge. It was said that a face full of icy water from his bucket would restore the wits of any player. A perpetual cigarette dangled from his lips, the smoke mingling with the pungent aroma of Wintergreen and sweaty bodies to create a cocktail which was the hallmark of the Rovers pavilion. Horses, dogs and humans were all the same to Willie who had more ways of making a few shillings than anyone would ever know about. Training greyhounds and working for bookies at a race course were two of them but Rovers directors had always turned a blind eye because Willie was a faithful servant, more so these days when he was giving his services free of charge to help out the team. With no coaching skill he was a staunch member of the school of thought which advocated 'Get stuck in, tackle owt in a different coloured jersey' and believed in 'big forrards and backs what can shift'. As a trainer to the local Harriers running club his methods didn't vary at the rugby ground; two laps of the pitch, a few sprints, and a game of 'tick' rugby and, more often than not, a pint or two with the players at the local. To walk out on the sacred turf of Wembley Stadium had been the highlight of his life, the memory sustained him through the club's bad times. He was worth having around for his sense of humour alone but even he was finding it hard to make the players laugh in the present circumstances. They were painfully aware that they were the 'whipping boys' of the league and the prospect of a game against the mighty Wigan didn't fill them with joy.

Willie was rubbing horse liniment into 'butcher' Bradley's thighs. 'Butcher' had worked a night shift down the pit and had only had three hours sleep. Working in a crouched position in a tunnel had aggravated an injury he had received the week before.

'Go easy Willie I'm not one of your ruddy dogs down at the track!" groaned 'butcher'. As the rod-like fingers sank into his muscles Willie grinned and the craggy forward pleaded for mercy. The ferretty little trainer rubbed all the harder. "Are you doubting my ability lad? I'm good at humans, dogs and hosses. Did I ever tell you I was employed by an eastern potentate to rub the women down in his harem? You see he thought I were a eunoch, mind you I would have been if he'd found out but he never did. I'd have had to make out my last will and tecticle if he had." Even little Willies outrageous tales couldn't bring a smile to the faces of the Rovers players whose only thoughts were on the match.

Len Grundy, the Rovers' captain and pack leader had called the players together for a talk before the chairman made his appearance in the dressing room to give the players his usual pep talk prior to the game, and to wish them well. Len was the only player left in the team who had played at Wembley. He was still a hard man, but his legs were no longer able to do his rugby brain justice. He knew that the team wasn't good enough, but he still hoped that they could keep on struggling until local talent could stiffen the ranks. The side was made up by cast-offs from other clubs, and players who had graduated from the A team, and could, in all honesty, only be described as honest to goodness triers. And yet if they had all been internationals, they could not have been any more loyal to the club. Len suggested that they played against Wigan without payment. To a man they agreed, even though they knew it would be considered as foolish loyalty by their wives and families.

"It might be the last game we ever play together, lads." he told his men, as they stripped for the match. "Let's go out there and play our hearts out. Forget who we're playing, just tackle everything in a cherry and white jersey." Len hadn't forgotten that they had a trialist in the team, he put his big arms around his shoulders and said "You're welcome here, lad. Best of luck."

When Joshua arrived in the dressing room, he was told the news. It was clearly an emotional shock to him. A large tear trickled down his

'BITING? WHAT ME REF?'

cheek. "What can I say, lads, only thank you! Make it a good clean gentlemanly game, but don't forget, if anyone gets carried off on a stretcher, make sure it's one of them!" Always send them out laughing had been his motto, but as he watched the back of the last player disappear down the tunnel he had to dry his eyes with his handkerchief. The line between laughter and tears was never so fine as at that moment.

The 'Entry Of The Gladiators' was rousingly played by the town brass band as Rovers ran onto the field. When Wigan ran out they were greeted by good natured boos and cat calls, as was the referee. No one expected anything else. The banter came thick and fast as the excitement of the crowd worked up to fever pitch.

"Just look at that big prop of Wigin's! I'd like to see him hanging on a butcher's hook."

"He's built like a shithouse door!"

"By gum, he's got a right pair of child bearing hips, has lad."

The Wigan speccies weren't slow to take up the verbal cudgels.

"He's etten half-backs for breakfast, has that lad. He goes to Bellevue Zoo and wrestles with gorillas and apes to keep his hand in."

"I'll bet his wife thinks he's up to monkey business." answered Albert, bringing an avalanche of groans.

"Come on Rovers, give 'em some bloody clog! They're only a gang o' girls. Up Rovers! Up Rovers! Get 'em fettled!"

The chant was taken up by the home supporters, and the stamping of feet in the popular stand must have sounded like the beating of jungle drums to the opposition. Where there's life there's hope and even though every home supporter, man, woman and child knew in their hearts that the Rovers had as much chance as a milkman's horse in the Grand National, they were still as eager as ever to shout them on.

From the kick off the ball was caught by little Dodger Dean on the right wing, who ran it open for it to pass through many pairs of hands before it was finally given to Billy Burden on the right wing, who scored in the corner. The home crowd roared. Joe Clare kicked a marvellous conversion from the touch-line. Could the Rovers spring the surprise of the year? From the restart, Len Grundy got his scrum-half going, who shot through the Wigan ranks as if they weren't there. He looked for support from his stand-off, but Walker-Smythe was far too slow to take advantage, and punted the ball weakly into the safe hands of Jim Sullivan. Soon the ball was back with the Rovers again, and it was the turn of 'butcher' Bradley to plunge deep into the ranks of the Wigan forwards. Len Grundy was playing like a lion and leading his men on by example as the Rovers monopolised the play, taking the game to the opposition with enthusiasm and skill. A wide pass from Grundy made an opening for Walker-Smythe who was far too slow to take advantage of it. He was grassed unceremoniously, and to make matters worse, he lost the ball. Joshua jumped to his feet in the best stand. "I thought you said he were a flyer!" he thundered at Stanley. "He should have been under the posts..... oh, bloody hell fire! He's knocked on again! Where the hell do you get 'em from, Stanley?"

"It's Dai Morgan you should be cussing, not me." said the aggrieved scout.

"He's not here, you are mate! Open line and he drops it."

The knock-on had occurred under the posts with a certain try for the taking; angry abuse was hurled at the new player. From the resulting scrum, the pass from Thomas the scrum-half was a beauty. Again, Walker-Smythe put it to ground. Despite the set backs and mistakes, the Rovers swarmed to the Wigan line in a green and yellow wave. Wigan were back pedalling, amazed by the fury of the onslaught.

Budgie Clarke took a long pass to weave and dodge his way deep into the Wigan ranks. For once he got a round of applause. His nickname was given to him because he was always getting the bird. The crowd were shouting their heads off, as a quick play-the-ball sent Ike Fishlock through a gap, only for him to be tackled inches short of the line. Walker-Smythe was the first receiver, and if he had been handed a bomb, he couldn't have been more terrified. His pass went to a Wigan player who set up a counter attack. It was soon discovered that his tackling was as poor as his passing and handling. 'Darkie' Bennet, the Wigan stand-off, brushed him off as if he was a flake of snow on his mackintosh. He sent his three quarters roaring into action, and it was now Wigan's turn to batter the Rovers' line. That weak tackle really incensed the connoisseurs of defensive play. "He's as much bloody use as a girl guide in a gym slip." roared Albert, jumping up and down in his excitement.

"He's a ponce! I told thee he'd be no bloody good, Albert." shouted Ambrose. The insults were interspersed with the standard slanging

'ROVERS PROP NEVER SHAVED FOR THREE DAYS BEFORE A MATCH'

remarks heard on every ground throughout the league.

"Get buggers on side, ref!"

"Yon ref needs a white stick. I reckon he's a Wiganer!"

"Put the ref a cherry and white jersey on!"

"Have you lost your pea ref?"

"Boo, boo....boo....boo.....boo!" roared the kids' pen, as the Wigan forwards tore into the Rovers' pack. When Jim Sullivan took a penalty, he was faced with more boos and jeering from the kids whose pen was situated directly behind the goal posts. The ice cool Sullivan slotted over the two points. Gallant though the Rovers were playing, Wigan were gradually taking hold of the game, and it was no surprise when Hector Gee tore past Walker-Smythe to set up a splendid passing movement which resulted in Alf Ellaby flying down the wing to beat the full back with a superb sidestep. The Rovers' diehards at the pavilion end roared for a forward pass. "It were a tuppenny bus ride forrard, open your eyes, ref!" shouted a solo voice.

Sullivan converted to make it 7 points to 5 to Wigan. This remained the score as the players trooped off at half time. The opinion on the terraces and in the stands was that the Rovers had played their hearts out and should have been in the lead. The unfortunate ex-Harlequin was being called the biggest wash-out ever to be seen in a Rovers' jersey. For once Joshua stayed away from the dressing room. He was frightened of what he might say. Instead, he found solace in the contents of his brandy flask.

The popular side terrace was a steep embankment made from cinders and colliery waste. Men who had loaded themselves full of ale before the match were too lazy to go the lavatory. Besides, it was an evil smelling place, far too small and usually swimming in the overflow from the metal receptacles. Instead, they urinated where they stood. Steam rose in the rarefied air, as the sea of urine ran down the bank to seep onto the pitch through the decrepit wooden fence. The stench didn't dampen the appetite of the regulars on the terrace. Pork pies, crisps and dripping butties were wolfed down hungrily, and those speccies lucky enough to own a thermos flask drank hot tea which added steam to the fetid vapour rising from the cinders. This tradition, nauseating though it was, was parallelled upon the pitch by another tradition, namely the playing of the 'Poet And Peasant' overture by the brass band. Even the noisiest spectator kept quiet as the music was played, imitating the reverent behaviour of a Wembley crowd when 'Abide with Me' is played. The 'Pullet and Pheasant' as the overture was colloquially known, rang out like an anthem of defiance, yet even the most optimistic Rovers supporter knew in his heart that it could be the last time they would hear it.

The second half began with a kicking duel between Sullivan and 'Cowboy' Smith. The idea of this aspect of the game was to find tↄuch, and to give the forwards a rest, as well as to gain territorial advantↄge, and there was always the chance of one of the full-backs forcing ↄis opposite number into making an error. After a couple of minutes 'Cowboy' decided it was better to make a break than trade kicks with the great Sullivan. As he ran with the ball, a Wigan forward was heading for him, hell for leather, unable to stop. He hit 'Cowboy' with a late tackle which insenced the Bramfield supporters. The incident occurred just below the best stand. Joshua and company were on their feet roaring at the referee. "Get the dirty sod off." yelled Bob Kearsley, waving his fist. 'Cowboy' was holding his arm in agony, and the touch judge was tearing towards the referee waving his flag. The referee called the Wigan man over and showed him 'Cowboy's' arm.

"He's bitten him, the dirty devil, bloody cannibal, he is!" yelled brother Bob. The forward opened his mouth wide, there wasn't a tooth in his head.

"It must have been a bloody vicious suck then, get him off." yelled Joshua. "He needs an early bath does that lad."

The referee decided that the tackle was fair, and awarded a scrum, and in doing so, became the world's most unpopular man. The derisive catcalls and slow hand claps went on for a full half-minute. A fierce forward battle ensued with some good old-fashioned foot dribbling from both sets of 'steam pigs' as they call the forwards in Yorkshire. Young Ken Gee and 'Mauler' Manley, the two open side props, broke away from a scrum to have a set-to. Gee was rubbing his face, obviously in some pain as blood ran down his chin. Manley never shaved for three days before a game, allowing a sharp stubble to grow, so he could rub it into the face of the opposing prop.

Although Rovers struggled manfully on, Ellaby was soon in for his second try. Walker-Smythe fielded a ball on the halfway line, a catch which was greeted with hoots of exaggerated astonishment and attempted a run, completely ignoring his support. He was grabbed by Sullivan, lifted up as if he were a baby, and dumped like a sack of coal. 'Woodbine' Willie ran on with his enamel bucket of icy cold water and magic sponge which was slopped into the face of the reeling stand-off. This was the cue for slow hand clapping and cries of "Off, off, off."

"That'll larn him to play with the big lads." shouted Albert.

"Take him back to his bloody nanny and change his nappy while you're at it." yelled Bert. "He's bleedin' nesh."

It is not my wish as a scribe to dwell upon the drubbing handed out to the Rovers, so I will not chronicle the rest of the match in painful detail. Suffice to say that the gallant has-beens and young lads of Bramfield went down like chaff before the scythe of Wigan. Ellaby ran in another two, the elusive Morley on the other wing scored a couple inside two minutes. Despite the Wigan pressure, Smythe-Walker was given a glorious opportunity to score in the dying seconds, but couldn't hold the pass. The whistle sounded and the score-board read:

Rovers 10   Wigan 33

An almost stony silence prevailed as the home crowd wound its way from the ground like a funeral procession, for in their hearts they knew that their beloved Rovers were dead. They were too sad to be angry. What was the point anyway? The inevitable loomed before them like an ogre. Even the Wigan crowd were quiet as if out of respect. Despite being an opposing side they didn't want to see the Rovers go out of the game. There is a camaraderie in rugby league and true lovers of the game get little satisfaction in seeing a team getting hammered every week. That evening an even deeper depression than ever hung over the town of Bramfield. It seemed that fate was playing them yet another dirty trick. This working class town of decent hard working folks, forced to exist hardly above the poverty line, deserved some sunshine in their drabness and austerity. Gloom and despair, already rooted in many hearts and souls, bit even deeper as the sad realisation that the Rovers were folding up sank in. There was little jollity in the pubs that night.

Chapter Twelve

The Final Whistle

It would take a tragedian endowed with the word craft of the bard of Avon, or a poet charged with the dramatic eloquence of a Tennyson to fully do justice to the dramatic upheaval which raged in the heart and soul of Joshua Hepplethwaite. As a humble scribe, I shall not even try. Let me simply state that his world had crumbled around him, and have done with it. One swallow does not make a summer. Neither does one good gate pull a rugby league club away from the brink of bankruptcy. The extra money taken at the turnstiles would be swallowed up next week when the team travelled to Hull for the cup tie. He couldn't expect his lads to play without pay again. He must face facts, and he must act. The trialist's saga had been another fiasco, the morale at the club was low enough, now the whole town would be throwing scorn at directors who had allowed such an inept player to take the field. After this, folks might even believe the paper story of a hooker playing with a wooden leg. Who could blame them if they did? The directors had always had the sympathy of their supporters throughout the club's bad times, but this latest debacle was stretching that loyalty to the limit. It was spitting in their faces.

Joshua had driven straight home from the ground, he didn't feel up to talking to the players. They had played their hearts out and he felt proud of them. He would make sure that each of them received a letter of thanks along with an official statement of the club's closure. He would notify the league's headquarters in Leeds on monday morning. As he sat head in hands by the parlour fire his wife made the tea, contemplating her husband's sorry state, when a knock on the front door interrupted her brown study.

"I'll go, Josh lad. You stay where you are. Keep warm." She returned shortly with an anxious look on her face. "You'll never guess who it is luv."

"Bank manager? Appen a lynching mob?"

"No.... Dai Morgan, the old player, and he's got Stanley Keighley with him, and that odd wife of his, and a young couple as well. And what's more, Bob and Bert Kearsley have just pulled up in a car."

If she had announced that Primo Scala and his accordion band were at the door, Joshua couldn't have been more dumbfounded. "Well, I'll go to our ouse! What the hell does Morgan want? Has he come to gloat or summat? What the hell is going on?"

"What shall I do, Josh luv? We can't leave 'em on the step."

"Why not?" asked Joshua.

"Well, what shall I say, luv?"

"Take 'em into the front room, but don't offer 'em any tea. Think on. It's not a cafe."

It was a grim faced Joshua who eventually joined the company in the front room. Not a word was spoken until Bob Kearsley cleared his throat:

"Joshua. Mr Morgan has got something to say. He was hoping to speak to you after the match. I knew you weren't very well, so I brought them all round here. I'm told it's very important news for the club."

"If you've got something to say, Mr Morgan, then say it." said Joshua coldly, standing by the piano. Morgan's voice had a nervous edge to it. He had known the chairman long enough to realise that he was very angry and upset.

"Mr Hepplethwaite, you know I played several seasons with the Rovers, and I assure you I would never do anything to harm the club, or to offend the wonderful supporters and people of Bramfield who made me so welcome. When I read that ridiculous article in the paper, I realised just how bad the situation was. I hatched a plot with my colleague here."

He pointed to Walker-Smythe, who had an arm in a sling and a swelling under one eye. "This is Jim Cadwallader, and he's a feature writer on the Daily Messenger. He's always been fascinated by rugby league, and loves to listen to my stories about the game. He wants todo

98

a feature on the sport, and to tell the story of Bramfield Rovers. So together we hatched a plot to fool Mr Keighley....."

"Not a difficult job." commented Joshua wryly.

Cadwallader now took up the story.

"I wanted to try it for myself, so I could write first hand about the game." Joshua was impressed.

"You're a brave 'un. I'll say that lad. Not to mention being a bit crazy. You didn't half take some hammer. And all that to write a story?"

"The punishment I took on the field was pretty ferocious, but I'd sooner go through all that than have to sit in that dressing room at half time with the players. I was about as popular as the butonic plague. My paper, Mr Hepplethwaite...."

"Bloody hell! He's got the name right." Interrupted Joshua, brightening up. Cadwallader pulled out his wallet with his free hand, and Dai took out a cheque and handed it to Joshua. Cadwallader continued. "The paper has asked me to give you this for the club. They want to sponsor the survival of the Rovers. It's a publicity stunt of course, but it'll help the club to survive." The chairman stared at the cheque.

"Five hundred quid! It must be me birthday."

"And that's not your only present." said Dai Morgan. "Here's another cheque." Joshua read the details aloud, almost unable to believe what was happening. "Pay Bramfield Rovers, R.L.F.C., five hundred pounds. It's from the Bramfield Trumpet, signed by Clarence Sneem. Well, I'll be blowed! I can't believe it. Why the hell should he give us money? Has he become a philantropist all of a sudden?" Dai Morgan laughed. "Not really, he's not changed. You see, him and I had a little chat. I've never liked him. He once wrote in his paper that I should give up rugby and take up singing professionally. Several of the players have threatened to thump him over the years. Snidy Sneem, we called him. He sent his article to our editorial office. He'd never dream that there was an ex-Rovers man working there. I confronted him today before the match. I gave him no option. "Pay up, or else our paper would expose him for the dirty little snake that he is. He was petrified."

Stanley Keighley went purple in the face. "I'll break his ruddy neck! I'll throttle t'bugger! I'll swing for t'swine!"

"You'll do no such thing, Stanley." admonished Joshua. "You'll swallow your anger and say nowt. We'll take his brass, that's what

99

we'll do. You lay one finger on him, and he'll have you in court, lad. Furthermore, he'll cancel the cheque. By the cram! It's like a fairy story, is this. I'll go to the foot of our stairs!"

Bob Kearsley shook his hand warmly. "Aye, it is an' all, Joshua, owd sprout. Happy ever after, that's us. That's how all good fairy stories should end. Are you feeling better now, me old mate? We can make a go of it after all! A thousand quid!"

"I am an'all. We'll paint the town red tonight, and we'll start out by going to Arkwright's U.C.P.[9]. The treat's on me. Then we'll come back here and knock hell out of the old Joanna." He put his expansive arms around Jim Cadwallader and his girlfriend. "You've made a poorly man very happy, and I'm suddenly very hungry. Come on, let's go."

"I've got an idea, Mr Hepplethwaite." said Clara. "Why don't we go to the King's Head?"

"Where's the King's Head, Clara lass?" asked Joshua.

"On the top of his shoulders!" exploded Clara in a high pitched giggle. "By the hell!" said Joshua. "Another bloody miracle. Clara Keighley's cracked a joke." Even Stanley laughed.

"By gum, it's wonderful." he said. I'll be able to go to Wales, scouting again like old times."

"Aye... lad." agreed Joshua cautiously. "But I'm coming with you."

"Aye, appen you better." said Clara. "Keep an eye on my Stanley." She squeezed her husband's hand, then kissed him on the cheek.

"By the heck Stanley, you're on a promise!" said Joshua aghast.

"'Appen so." said Stanley. But when his eye had caught the alluring glimpse of his wife's baggy khaki stockings, he said "but appen not."

"Have a pickle instead." said Bob Kearsley, getting his jar out.

And the Rovers did live, and play, happily ever after.

NOTES

1	CH1	The old name for the game.
2	CH1	Old name for urine. Old folks used it for corns and other foot problems.
3	CH1	Famous colourful character, tipster on race courses. "I gotta 'orse!" was his well known chant.
4	CH2	Three notorious Forwards who played for St Helens Recs in the twenties and early thirties. Known as the "Three Musketeers" On the fence of City Road ground was painted "SMITH FILDES and MULVANNEY. MANGLING DONE HERE!
5	CH6	Known as the Lancashire Caruso Burke sang with Madame Melba at Covent Garden in 1919 and became famous for a short spell. A rugby league supporter, he returned to Leigh and it is claimed that he was one of the early pioneers of the rugby league coupons.
6	CH7	A many legged contraption for agitating the clothes when they were in the boiler. Fore runner of the spinner in modern washing machines.
7	CH7	A Preston man who stuttered. He was a lay preacher who was dead against drink. His stuttering caused him to give the word tee-total to the language. "t—— t—— tee—— total abstinence!"
8	CH8	Famous Saints and Great Britain stand off.
9	CH12	United Cow Products – – famous for tripe, cow heels and other succulent northern dishes.

Key to grounds listed on front and back covers.

Craven Park Duke Street	Barrow
Mount Pleasant	Batley
Odsal	Bradford
McClaren Field	Bramley
Gillford Park	Carlisle
Wheldon Road	Castleford
Victory Park	Chorley (shared with Chorley A.F.C.)
Mount Pleasant	Dewsbury (shared with Batley)
	Batley)
Tattersfield	Doncaster
Post Office Road	Featherstone
Crystal Palace	Fulham
Thrum Hall	Halifax
Hoghton Road	Highfield (St Helens)
Fartown	Huddersfield
Boulevard	Hull
Craven Park Preston Road	Hull K.R.
Elland Road	Hunsley (shared with Leeds A.F.C.)
Lawkholme Lane	Keighley
Bass Headingley	Leeds
Hilton Park	Leigh
Harvey Hadden Stadium	Nottingham City
Watersheddings	Oldham
Spotland	Rochdale
South Rydale Stadium	Ryedale – York
Knowsley Road	St Helens
City Road (as in novel)	St Helens Recs (now
	defunct)
The Willows	Salford
McCain Stadium	Scarborough Pirates
Don Valley Stadium	Sheffield Eagles
Station Road	Swinton
The Arena Princess St.	Blackpool Gladiators
Belle Vue	Wakefield Trinity
Wilderspool	Warrington
Recreation Ground	Whitehaven
Naughton Park	Widnes
Central Park	Wigan
Derwent Park	Workington
Marl Heights	Bramfield Rovers
	Pardon? Who are they?

Read the Book and Find Out!